MARY BROWN IS LEAVING TOWN

BERNICE BLOOM

FOREWORD

Hello,

Thank you so much for choosing 'Mary Brown is leaving town' - a book in which our gorgeous heroine heads off to a health spa with her mother, only to discover that this is not a sun-soaked retreat with facials and massages but a military-style boot camp.

She's stuck in Portugal with ferocious instructors dressed in army fatigues and a bunch of super-fit recruits.

How will she cope?

And how will she cope when she returns from the camp to the realisation that her relationship with Ted is over? Will she wallow in misery, or will she set out on a whole load of increasingly ridiculous internet dates? I think you know the answer to that!

I hope you love the book,

Bernie xx

PS Please note that this book was previously released as 'Adorable Fat Girl goes to Weight Loss camp' and 'Adorable Fat Girl goes internet dating'. If you have read either of those two books, you have already read this.

NOTHING BUT CARROTS

I was all curled up on mum's sofa, clutching a sweet cup of tea and feeling its warmth against the palms of my hands as the rain hammered against the windows. It had been pouring all day and was now coming down so hard that you could hear it hitting the conservatory roof like gunfire. Darkness had started to descend. It was only 7 pm, for God's sake. Outside it looked like the end of the world.

"I should go home soon," I said. "But this rain is just awful. I can't face going out in it."

"No, don't be ridiculous. You can't go anywhere til it stops. Just relax and enjoy your tea. Stay for something to eat, and your dad will run you back later."

"Thanks, mum," I said, snuggling further into the sofa and feeling all safe and secure. The theme tune for the One Show came on, and I don't think I'd ever felt cosier in my life. I clutched my mug between my hands and blew onto the scalding liquid, watching the steam fly up onto my face, warming my nose. It was like I was giving myself a mini steam facial.

"How are things going then?" asked mum, eying me with confusion as I tried to get the steam to hit my chin, where I'm particularly prone to blackheads. "What on earth are you trying to do with that mug?"

"Nothing," I said, continuing to hold the mug in position. You'd pay £40 for this sort of treatment at the beauticians.

"You seem a bit out of sorts. Is everything OK with you and Ted?"

I shrugged, not because things weren't going well with my boyfriend but because I now had my chin right over the top of the mug and didn't want to move.

"For the love of God, are you having some sort of breakdown over there? Or are you trying to drink your tea through your chin?"

"Neither," I said, reluctantly putting down the mug. "I was just warming up my chin."

"Warming up your chin?"

"Yes. My chin was cold, that's all." I crossed my arms over my chest and turned to watch the television. They had just started a segment about window boxes.

"You and Ted aren't getting on well, are you?" she said, her voice full of anxiety. "He's such a lovely man; it would be a shame if you messed this up."

"Things are fine," I replied, turning my attention back to the planting in the BBC studio. "He works long hours, and I've been away a lot recently, so we haven't seen all that much of one another, but everything's just fine."

"Oh," she said. "Doesn't sound like things are 'just fine' if you never see him. And 'fine' is such an odd word to use. I thought you two were in love. You came back from Lapland and said the two of you were moving in together. I thought I might have grandchildren by the end of the year."

"You might want to rethink that, mum."

"But you and Ted are OK? Why won't you talk to me about it?"

"We are. Honestly, mum, we're both doing well, and the relationship's great; I just want to see what they do with these primroses."

"OK," she said, taking a large gulp of tea, but she looked far from OK. She wanted to talk, but I genuinely wanted to see what they would put next to the primroses. I work in a gardening and DIY store and have been charged with sorting out all the window boxes next week. I need tips from Alan Titchmarsh.

Mum fell into a respectful silence while the colourful, floral creations took shape. Then the programme moved on to Phil Tufnell talking about the plight of urban foxes. Mum seized her moment and grabbed the remote control, hitting the pause button and leaving poor Phil frozen on the screen. I knew what was coming.

"Come on then," she said. "Tell me what the trouble is."

"There's no trouble. Honestly, mum. Ted and I are very happy."

"But there's no talk of you moving in together as you'd planned? No talk of wedding bells?"

"No talk like that at all, mum. But we're happy, so stop worrying."

"I do worry; I can't help it," she said. "You were always so sad and out of sorts until Ted came along...he's transformed you. He's a lovely man. I'd hate to see things going wrong."

"They won't. Everything's fine. Can we talk about something else, or I'll put the foxes back on."

"OK. You can talk to me anytime you want if you're worried about anything."

"I know," I said. "And I will if I'm worried about anything." Although the one thing I'm sure of is that my

3

mother would be the last person on the planet I'd talk to if I were having problems with my relationship.

"What are you up to, then?" she asked. "Any exciting trips planned?"

"Well, Ted and I are talking about going to America in the summer. He's looking at what sort of holiday we could do. I fancy a road trip - you know - take in a lot of places all in one visit. Route 66 and all that."

"I thought you were going somewhere else as well," said mum. "Like a health place or something?"

"Yes, I'm off on a weight loss retreat in Portugal next week. I told you all about that."

"A weight loss retreat. That's right," she mused, offering me a chocolate biscuit. I took one, of course. Always better to discuss the merits of weight loss retreats while dunking heavily-coated chocolate hobnobs into devilishly sweet tea.

"All they'll give you to eat at weight loss retreats is carrots. You do know that, don't you?"

"I'm sure that's not ALL we'll be given," I replied. "I'm sure there'll be other food."

"Nope...carrot juice, carrots in salads and carrots on their own - carrots lying on the plate in front of you, taunting you with their orangeness. By the end of the week, you'll be having nightmares about carrots taking over the country. Just talk to Aunty Susan, she went on a Fat Camp when she was 20, before her wedding, and she was definitely a light orangey colour when she came home. Take a look at the wedding photos. Looks like Donald Trump, she does."

"She does not. I've seen her wedding photos; she looks lovely in them."

"Lovely, yes, but apricot coloured. I mean, apricot is a nice colour for a blouse or a summer skirt, but not for your face. In the wedding photos, she looked like she's been living too close to a nuclear plant or bathing in cheesy wotsits."

"Well, even if it was all about carrots back then, it's not now. Also, it's definitely not called 'Fat Camp'. You're talking about something from the 1950s; it's all different today. I'm going on a weight loss retreat and will have healthy food, fresh air and exercise, and I'll come back energised and looking a lot like Jennifer Lawrence. It will be brilliant."

"Do you have to write about it again on that blog thing?"

"Yep," I said. "Another free trip."

I've got myself a nice little gig writing for my friend Dawn's blog. It's called 'Two Fat Ladies', and because I'm rather well-upholstered, she invites me to help her review various holidays; the trouble is - things always go wrong.

This is the third trip I've managed to wangle myself onto. I've been on safari (got stuck up a tree in my knickers, and it all ended up on webcam - disaster!) and went on a cruise (befriended a 90-year-old man and a dazzling dancer and managed to miss the ship and bump into an ex-boyfriend - disaster!).

I hope this one will be straightforward, and I'll come back looking thin and lovely without creating any colossal dramas along the way.

"Well, I hope you're right. I hope that fat camps have changed since your Aunty Susan went," said mum, with a raise of her eyebrows. A smile played upon her lips, and a look of furtive shame crept across her features. "It was funny, though, hearing all the stories. I remember Susan telling me about when she escaped and ran to the pub with one of the other women, and the pub landlord guessed what they'd done and called the Fat Camp owner, who sent out two guys to collect them and bring them back. They were even frisked back at Fat Club, and two packets of pork scratchings were found in your Aunty Susan's knickers. Don't tell her I told you that, though, will you? We called her piggy pants for ages afterwards...don't tell her I told you that either."

I smiled as I thought about my sensible aunty having pub snacks hidden in her girdle.

"I won't be like that," I said. "I want to go and do it properly and lose loads of weight so I can start on a proper health and fitness drive and get down to a healthy, sensible weight."

"Good girl," said mum. "You won't want another one of these, then."

Mum took a hobnob and bit into it slowly while I flicked through the weight loss camp brochure.

"Most people lose 7lbs on holiday," I read out.

"That'll be the carrots," she replied through a mouth full of biscuits. I ignored her and carried on reading.

"If you join the running group, you can expect to increase the speed and distance you can run dramatically."

"Yep, everyone is running away from carrots," she said.

"There's no mention of bloody carrots in the brochure. They talk about healthy, organic food that will fill you up and give you the strength you need to exercise while allowing you to shed all the weight you want."

"The carrots are a secret."

"For the love of God, mum. Shut up about the carrots."

A WEEK LATER, Aunty Susan came over for lunch with Uncle Mark, and I knew the subject of my pending Weight Loss holiday would be raised. Mum was dying to have her theories about the holiday confirmed.

"I was telling Mary about the Fat Camp that you went on before your wedding, Sue," she said.

"Oh God!" said Aunty Susan, dropping her cutlery, so it clattered on her plate. "That was terrible. Do you remember? That other lady and I tried to escape, but they came and caught us."

"I never knew about that," said Mark. "Where did you try to escape to?"

"To the pub and the fish and chip shop," replied Susan. "They caught us in the pub, I think, before we'd even had the chance to get to the fish and chip shop."

"Why would you try to escape?" Mark asked. "I thought you liked going to spas and things like that."

I braced myself.

"I love spas, but this place was dreadful...they made us exercise from 5 am til 8 pm and fed us nothing but carrots."

"You see," said mum, turning around to face me with a look of triumph on her face. "What did I tell you? Nothing but carrots."

MUM ON TOUR

*W*hile mum sat and explained to Aunty Susan how she'd been warning me about the carrots, my phone rang. Dawn's number appeared on the screen, so I excused myself and wandered into the kitchen.

"Hi Flairy, zits fawn," said Dawn's familiar voice.

"Sorry? I couldn't understand a word of that."

I could hear mum and Aunty Susan laughing uproariously as they told Uncle Mark about the Fat Camp she'd been on. They didn't mention her hiding pork scratchings in her knickers, though. I must make sure to mention that.

"It's Fawn," said the voice on the phone.

"Fawn?"

"No, Dawn. Sorry - I've got a mouthful of food."

"Not carrots, I hope."

"No, of course not. I'm eating cake. Why would you think I'd be eating carrots?"

"Just something my mum said earlier about everyone at weight loss camp eating nothing but carrots."

"Well, your mum will be able to find out for herself if she wants," said Dawn.

"What do you mean?"

"I mean, she will literally be able to find out for herself. The organisers of the weight loss camp say you can take your mum with you because they are keen to advertise a Mother's Day special that they are running next month. They thought that would make an interesting angle for the blog, and I agree with them, to be honest. You know, 'weight loss camp with my mum'. I think it could be hilarious for readers."

I was silent. I wasn't expecting this at all.

"Mary, are you still there?" asked Dawn.

"Yes, still here, but shocked into silence," I said. "I can't take my mum with me."

"Come on; it would make great copy. Can you imagine it...you're really witty, Mary, and have got a great following already. Weight-watching with your mum will add a whole new dimension to that. Readers will love it. Readers will think it's hilarious as they hear about the two of you."

"Yeah, funny for readers, but hell on earth for me."

"I'm sure your mum is lovely."

"She is," I said, as mum walked past me to get more drink. She pulled out a fresh bottle of sherry, and I realised they were in for a long night...when she and Aunty Susan get cracking on the sherry, there's no stopping them: they'll be dancing to Elvis and Buddy Holly in no time. It's even worse when her other sister, Mavis, comes over. The three of them are bonkers.

"But mum's not fat. I can't take my mum on a weight loss camp if she doesn't need to lose weight; that would be crazy."

"Ooooooo..." said mum, stopping in the doorway with her bottle of sherry and spinning round to face me. "Yes, you can take me to weight loss camp with you. I need to lose a few pounds. Everyone over the age of 60 needs to lose weight. I used to be so slim and elegant. Not anymore, though. Take me with you, Mary; we'd have such fun."

"Let me talk this through with her, and I'll come back to you," I said to Dawn as I ended the call and followed mum into the sitting room. Mum was in there flexing her muscles at Aunty Susan. She had rolled up the short sleeves of her silk top and displayed arms with the merest hint of flabby skin hanging beneath them. This was supposed to indicate how overweight she was.

"Isn't it awful," she said to Aunty Susan as she gently nudged her arm and shook her head as it rippled. "However slim you keep yourself, you can't help it when you get older.

"I wouldn't worry, mum; I've got more loose flesh than that on my fingers," I said.

"So, am I coming?"

"I don't think it will be your sort of thing," I tried. "When have you ever shown any interest in health and fitness?"

"Excuse me, Madam, but when have you?" asked mum.

I nodded at her. She had a point. Though, in my defence, I talk a lot about getting fit...I don't do anything about it. Does it count if you talk about it endlessly?

"I took up yoga," I said, remembering my weekend retreat a while ago. "I wore nothing but bloody Lycra for days."

"Well, that's true," said mum. "But how much yoga did you do? It sounds like you spent most of the time falling over and ogling men in tight shorts."

Again, she wasn't wrong.

"I think it would be lovely if we went to the weight loss camp together. I understand if you say you don't want me to go with you, but I'd like to."

"Ah, go on, Mary, take her," said Aunty Susan. "She'll be very well-behaved."

Oh God, why was this so hard?

"But remember what you said about the carrots," I said. "You wouldn't want to eat carrots for every meal, would you?"

"I wouldn't mind," said mum. "I wouldn't mind what I ate as long as I was with you."

Bugger, bugger, bugger. What could I possibly say to that?

"Of course, I'd like you to come, mum," I told her with a heavy heart. I'd imagined myself frolicking on the beach with handsome instructors and flirting outrageously with the tennis coaches before sneaking out for late-night glasses of wine with the other guests, not to mention the snacks I was planning to take. Now it looked like it was going to be all fitness classes and games of Scrabble.

"Ooo, what fun," mum said. "Don't worry about a thing now, Mary. I'll be there to keep you on the straight and narrow and out of trouble."

"That's what I'm worried about," I said.

FIVE DAYS before the weight loss retreat, I was trying so hard to be good. I didn't want to look like a pot-bellied pig in my bikini. Going with mum added a new level of stress to the trip; she was so lovely and slim - I didn't want everyone to look at us both and wonder why on earth I was so huge when she was so tiny. I thought that if I lay off the booze and cut back on the snacks, I'd look a bit better…just a bit.

"I'm not going to drink tonight," I said to Ted, refusing a glass and taking a sip of his wine when his back was turned. "I'm going to be good."

"Um…" said Ted, having seen me stealing his glass from the corner of his eye. "For someone who's not going to drink tonight, you seem to be drinking a lot of my wine."

"Everyone knows that calories taken off someone else's plate or from someone else's glass don't count," I advised.

"Right," said Ted, looking highly dubious.

"It's a flawless plan, to be fair," I said, taking another large sip from his glass.

"Just have a glass of wine if you want a glass of wine, woman," he said. "You're not going to get any fatter drinking your glass instead of mine."

God love him; does he know nothing?

"By the way, what are you doing tomorrow? Do you fancy coming to the football with me?" he said. "There's a group of us going; it will be a laugh."

"I'd rather sit at home and stick pins in my eyes - why would I want to go to the football?"

"All the other girlfriends go," he said in a whiny voice. "They talk among themselves; you don't have to watch the football...just come along and have a beer and mix with everyone."

"Next time," I said. "I'm going holiday shopping with mum tomorrow to get supplies for our trip." Heaven help me; I'm not sure which is the worse day out - football with Ted and his lager lout friends or clothes shopping with mum.

"Blimey, are you sure you wouldn't rather come to the football?"

"I have to go with her," I said. "If I don't, it will be an utter disaster. Yesterday she was talking about buying a jazzy pink headband and ankle warmers to wear to the fitness classes. If I don't take her in hand, she'll look like Jane Fonda's grandmother. I need to go with her to ensure she doesn't lose her mind in Sports Direct."

"OK, well - rather you than me - if you change your mind, come down to the football - you know where we'll be."

"I will," I said. The awful thing was, I didn't want to go to the football. I don't like the sport, and I don't feel like making an effort with Ted because he never makes any effort with me. I know that sounds ridiculously childish, but he works all the time, goes out with his football mates and doesn't have much time for me. Whenever we see one another, he's too tired to go out, so we sit around in our slobby jogging bottoms, drinking wine.

THE NEXT DAY I woke with a heavy heart at the thought of the delights ahead of me. My mum is lovely, she really is, and I'm sure your mum is too, but would you want to go on holiday with her? Honestly? And would you want to go shopping for fitness wear with her before the holiday? You don't need to answer that; we all know the answer.

I took the bus to mum's house in Esher first thing in the morning and picked her up, and then the two of us went on the bus into Kingston. She was so chirpy and thrilled at the idea of going shopping with me that I felt terrible about all the things I'd been thinking about. I decided to be positive and upbeat and make this experience something mum would love.

"Where shall we go first?" asked mum. Her cheeks were flushed, and she looked excited that we were out on a shopping trip. I swear you'd think I never went anywhere with her or that she had never been shopping. "I suppose you'll want to go to Topshop or Zara - or some of those other young person's shops, won't you?" she said. "I'll come with you, but I need to get my clothes somewhere a little more age-appropriate."

I didn't want to tell mum that the clothes in Topshop hadn't fitted me since puberty, and I hadn't been in Zara since I got stuck in a dress there and ended up ripping it to get it off.

"I was thinking about the department stores - John Lewis and Bentalls, and maybe Marks and Spencer," I said. I knew they were the most likely shops to stock a swimming costume that was big enough for me. I also needed a cover-all kaftan, so I didn't scare the locals and a summery dress in case of a cocktail party one evening. "Do those shops sound OK?"

"Yes, very nice," she said, delighted with my suggestions. "And we don't have to worry about paying for lunch because I've bought sandwiches with me." She opened her bag to reveal clingfilm-wrapped bread at the bottom and a flask."

"That's soup in there. It's Heinz, so it should be nice. And I've got boiled eggs for us to have with the sandwiches. They're here, somewhere."

"Great," I said as mum rummaged around on her egg hunt. "We'll go to the park after shopping for a picnic."

Mum brightened further at the thought of that.

We decided to go to Sports Direct first, mainly because we walked right past it when we got off the bus, but also because mum wanted trainers and dad had persuaded her that the only decent place to buy trainers was a sports shop.

"Your father says that I mustn't buy cheap ones from a supermarket, I've got to buy proper ones from a sports shop, or I'll slip and break my hip or something."

"OK," I said, and in we went. Mum tried on a succession of shoes, and as she skipped around the shop, testing them out, I thought how youthful she looked - she was very young-looking for her age and didn't have an ounce of fat on her.

"I think I'll take these pink ones," she said with a girlish smile. "Shall I get you some too?"

"I'd look ridiculous in them," I said. "I only wear black trainers."

"Well, I think you should get some brightly coloured ones. You'd look lovely in these."

"No, mum, honestly, it's kind of you, but last time I wore pink, I looked like Tinky Winky, so I've stopped all bright colours until I lose weight."

"Let me buy you something," said mum. "Choose whatever you fancy as a treat from me."

I didn't want to buy anything in the sports shop. Nothing looks more ridiculous than a woman who's not done a moment's exercise since the 1990s, all dressed up in brand new exercise gear, especially if the gear is three sizes too small…. which it would have been if I'd attempted to buy something in there.

After the shoe shopping, we went upstairs, and mum bought some lovely, deeply-flattering Lycra sportswear. I can't tell you how annoying it is when your mum looks better in clothes than you. I could have hit her as she emerged from the changing rooms saying: "Could you get one of these for me in size 10, Mary? This one's far too big for me."

As I watched her, I kept thinking, 'why am I fat, and she's not?' I mean - how does the whole overeating thing work? You'd think I would be fat because my mum is fat, and she overfed me from a young age or gave me a negative relationship with food or something. But it doesn't seem to work like that - I seem unable to stop eating and thinking about eating, whereas mum eats when she's hungry.

Our relationships with food are so different. It's like food means a different thing in our lives - to me, it's a joyous thing hovering on the horizon, never quite out of sight, always alluring and always exciting. When there's food in the room, it's like I become possessed…I can't relax til it's all eaten, and when I eat it, it's like I can't get enough of it, like no amount of food's ever going to satisfy me, ever going to fill me up and allow me to relax. I wish I didn't have to eat ever again. I wish eating weren't part of life.

"Right," said mum, returning to me with all her purchases packed in a carrier bag. "Let's go and have a picnic in the park, shall we?"

"Oooh yes," I said, trotting along beside her, my maudlin mood lifted a little by the thought of food (see what I mean? It's insane).

"Shall we walk down to the grassy bank we went past on the bus a little earlier? It seemed nice there, didn't it?"

"Or we could go just here," I said, indicating a small park that was not as nice as the spot mum was talking about but was nearer, meaning we could eat sooner, and I wouldn't have to walk for ages.

"I thought the spot by the river was nicer?"

"No - the ducks and geese come there, and they're vicious," I said. "This will be much better." I threw down my coat as a makeshift blanket before mum could attempt to make me change my mind.

"OK," she said and started unloading the picnic. I felt instantly bad for making her sit there. I'm just horrible when there's food around.

"We can go back to the river if you like," I said.

"No, said mum, opening a tiny packet of sandwiches. "Don't worry. This is just perfect."

SOLDIERING ALONG

*T*he flight left on a Monday while Ted was at work (of course), so the task of taking two women and bags full of leisurewear to the airport fell to dad.

"Now, have you both got everything," he said once we were in the car with our luggage in the boot. "Check now, before we leave."

We both rummaged through our respective handbags and said we were OK. We had our passports with us, and that's all that mattered.

"You don't need tickets?" asked dad.

"Err, no - it's all magic now," I said. "They are e-tickets - on my phone."

"Have you got the information about the camp and how we get there?" asked mum.

I pulled an envelope out of my bag. "All in here," I said. I hadn't opened it, but I knew it was all there. With that, we were off, chugging along the motorway on our journey to Heathrow.

. . .

AFTER CHECKING in and passing through security with an alarming lack of hassle or incident, mum and I headed for the beauty counters in the duty-free shop.

I sprayed a liberal amount of Chanel No5 onto my wrists and neck and tipped way too much body lotion into my hands so that I ended up spreading it up my arms to get rid of it. Mum was peering into a small mirror at the skincare counter next to me, wrinkling up her nose in disgust at the sight of herself. "You've no idea how bloody hideous it is," she said.

"How hideous what is, mum?" I replied. The lipstick she'd tried on seemed perfectly acceptable to me.

"Ageing... Waking up in the morning and discovering that your jawline has dropped so far that your jowls are resting on your shoulders, and your eyes have disappeared completely – hidden behind bags, wrinkles and a forehead that's dropped four inches."

I should tell you at this stage that mum is attractive; she is slim, elegant and always has perfect hair (You know how some people are like that... They always have gorgeous hair, whereas mine is hit and miss – regardless of what I do with it, sometimes it looks okay, and other times it looks terrible for no reason at all).

Anyway, I'm saying mum looks good, and she's not all that vain, so the little outburst as she peered into the mirror was a bit of a shock.

"You look great, mum; what are you talking about?"

"I'm talking about the unwanted hairs popping up on my chin, the grey roots and the beachball that has appeared where my waistline used to be. The only thing I've got in my favour is that I haven't got incontinence or piles, unlike Aunty Susan."

"Yeah, thanks, mum. I needed to know that."

"And the reason for that is because I do daily pelvic floor

exercises, which makes a world of difference. It would be best if you started now. I'll show you when we get to the room. Honestly, I do them so often it's a wonder I can't get my pelvic floor up to touch the back of my throat."

"Oh God, mum."

I turned to look at the mascaras. My eyes are the only part of me that I like. I have big eyes, you see. In fact, I have big everything, but big eyes are allowed. Have you ever thought about that? I have huge feet, and that's frowned upon. Having size eight feet is not ladylike. Having big thighs is not good, and neither is having a big tummy. But big eyes? That's good; that's allowed. A big smile is allowed too, but not a big neck.

I need to go and live in a country where all big is beautiful, and my vast arse is celebrated as much as my huge eyes. Maybe Tonga or somewhere. Isn't the King of Tonga chosen as king because he's the fattest person in the country? Christ, I'd be running the place in the blink of an eye.

I turned back to mum to find her holding her forehead up with her index fingers so that her eyebrows were raised, and she was pulling the sides of her face out with her thumbs.

"Do I look young?" she asked.

I didn't know what the right answer was. If I said "yes", that would imply that I thought she usually looked old, but if I said "No", she'd think that even when she rearranged her features with her fingers, she still looked old.

"You look startled," I told her. "Not a good look, if you don't mind me saying. Now come on, let's go and get a drink. I want to tell you about all my plans to move to Tonga."

It was only a quick visit to the pub (mum wasn't such a fan of all-day drinking as I'd hoped she'd be), then I rushed into Boots and bought more miniature toiletry items than either of us could reasonably get through in a decade, as well as stocking up on medical supplies for the flight in such quantities that we could have opened a small on-board hospital. Then it was time to board.

ON THE PLANE, I settled myself into my seat and nervously raised my hand to attract the attendant's attention.

"Can I help you?" she asked in a loud voice.

"I'll need a seatbelt extension, please," I said.

"A what?"

"A seat belt extender," I said, doing actions to mimic the putting on of a seatbelt rather than raise my voice.

"Of course, madam," she said, scurrying to find one.

"You don't need a seatbelt extender," said mum, valiantly rushing to my defence. "You're not that fat."

I love that she's so protective, but her loyalty verges on blindness.

"Shall we have a little drink on the plane?" I suggested.

"Tea?" she said.

"Gin?" I responded.

"Are you an alcoholic?" she asked.

"What? Because I fancy a little drink on the plane on the way to holiday?"

"No, because it's a weight loss camp, and only a nutcase would order alcohol on the way to it…. a nutter or someone who loved drinking so much they couldn't help themselves. Someone with a problem, perhaps?"

"It's going to be a long five days," I muttered as we both ordered tea. "A long, long time."

WE ARRIVED AT FARO AIRPORT, and I pulled the letter out of my bag to work out where we were supposed to be. I slid my finger along the seal and tore the envelope open, pulling out the pages inside.

"Let's see, it's called... 'Forces Fitness'," I said, noticing the military-style logo at the top of the information sheet.

"Forces fitness?" said mum. "What do you mean? Like military training? Drill sergeants and press-ups in the mud?"

Mum and I looked at one another.

"Forces Fitness? Shit," I said. "I thought it would be all fruit kebabs and sparkling elderflower juice. I don't fancy military fitness at all."

"It can't be," said mum. "Was there information with the letter? What does it say?"

"I didn't look," I confessed, flicking through all the other pages in the envelope, which announced that the camp was a military-style fitness experience.

"Oh God...look, mum."

Two men dressed in army fatigues were marching up to us, clutching clipboards. One of them was around my age and desperately handsome with chiselled features and big shoulders. He looked rugged and manly but had long eyelashes and sea-green eyes. He looked like he could handle himself in a fight, but he would also be nice to kittens and always remember your birthday. The other man was older and looked like he would crush kittens with his bare hands and force-feed them to you on your birthday. It was odd because the younger man was bigger and much stronger-looking but somehow had a warmth about him that was lacking in his mate. The older man snarled at me.

"Names?" he said as if I was a prisoner who'd just been captured. I felt like turning around and running back through security and onto the plane and demanding that it take me back to London. I couldn't face this week if it comprised of them shouting and calling me useless and hopeless to break me down. I'm broken enough; I need building, not breaking, for God's sake.

"Didn't you hear me?" he said. "I need your names and your passports to be surrendered."

"OK, well, I'm Mary, and this is my mum," I replied, directing my comment to the handsome man. "And why do we have to 'surrender' our passports? Are we being arrested or something?"

"Passports," he said.

Mum obediently rummaged in her handbag to find hers, but I wasn't interested in playing their silly games.

"I've told you our names; what are yours?"

"Staff A and Staff B," replied the man, adding: "We don't do first names."

Oh, God.

"Look, we only want to lose a few pounds. Neither of us plans to invade anywhere, and we do not want to fight anyone. I want a nice relaxing week."

"OK, Mary," he said, putting his face right next to mine in quite a threatening way. "We'll see what we can do. Follow me."

Mum and I half-walked, half-skipped behind the two men who strode out in front. The only compensatory factor was that the handsome man (who I think was Staff B) had the most incredibly tight bum.

I could see that mum was struggling beside me. She ran a little to keep up and moved her bag from one hand to the other. He could have offered to carry it for her. I know they're doing this whole 'tough guy' thing, but mum's not far off 70, for God's sake.

I took the bag out of mum's hand and carried it along with my own, struggling to keep up with them as they marched ahead. Then a very tall man appeared beside me. He was long and lean with round glasses and a mop of sandy blond hair.

"Let me take that," he said, relieving me of mum's bag. He

had a warm, friendly face and looked a little shy - unlike the other two guys.

"Do you work for the fitness camp," I asked, wondering why he wasn't all dressed up in army fatigues.

"No. I'm a guest," he said. "I'm Simon."

Oh, I see. "I'm Mary," I said, smiling at him. He had lovely warm eyes. There was something tender and likeable about him. He wasn't conventionally good-looking, but he had charisma. When he smiled, his whole face lit up. I noticed mum had speeded up and was talking to the fearsome-looking army guys.

"So, are you looking forward to this week?" I asked him. "To be honest, I'm terrified of what they're going to get us doing. I didn't realise it was a military fitness thing. I thought it would be Slimming World in the sunshine."

"You'll be fine," he said with a small laugh. "I mean - it's not quite Slimming World, but I'm sure you'll enjoy it. I've been on one of these camps before, and they're good fun once you get going. Don't worry. These guys act tough, but they're good at what they do, and if you listen to them, you'll lose a lot of weight and feel great by Friday."

I smiled at him adoringly and thought how much more fun this whole holiday would be now that I had someone to chat with and flirt with. Not that I fancied him...he just had a pleasant manner and liked me, which was lovely.

"Are you very fit?" I said. "If you don't mind me asking. I'm worried I won't be fit enough to keep up."

"Not really," said Simon. "I cycle daily, but I'm not super fit, so don't worry. On a camp like this, you'll find that there's always someone fitter than you and someone less fit than you."

I didn't imagine they'd find someone less fit than me, but I appreciated the comment, so I smiled happily at Simon and thanked him.

"Do you mind if I ask you something?" he said, looking a little embarrassed.

"Of course," I said, fluttering my eyelashes, delighted that I'd coated them in brown owl mascara at the airport.

"I'm always blunt when I see a lady I'm attracted to; I don't like to hang back."

"Oh," I said, feeling my heart beating faster. I knew he was going to ask whether I was single. I felt excited at the prospect, but what should I say? I was tempted to lie to keep the magic alive between the two of us; after all, things weren't going well with my boyfriend. It would make the week much more fun if I had someone to flirt with. So, I smiled encouragingly at Simon and flicked my hair girlishly.

"OK then. What did you want to ask me?"

"What I wanted to ask you was - who's that lady with you earlier, the one whose bag I'm carrying? She's beautiful."

What?

"THAT'S MY MUM!" I growled.

"Oh," he said. "Is your dad on the trip?"

"No," I replied. "But my mum and dad are still together, so keep your hands off her."

"OK," he said, looking shocked by my outburst. "But if your mum and dad ever split up, I'd be interested."

"Get away from me," I said, shooing him away. "Go on, shoo."

My bloody mother! What did it say for my attractiveness if men preferred my mum? Christ, this was going to be a marvellous few days.

FOUR VILLAS IN THE SUNSHINE

*W*e all climbed into the back of a small minibus. There was me, mum, Simon, who I had gone entirely off and was keen to keep as far from my mum as possible, and one of the army blokes (the handsome one). The older, angrier army guy had gone back to meet the rest of the group in his inimitable, gentle style. He arrived back a few minutes later with another couple of people: a woman called Karen and a guy named Graham.

Karen looked utterly terrified as she took her seat and looked up at the two army guys.

"They aren't as horrible as they look," I whispered to her, though I had no evidence for that - I just couldn't stand to see her looking so downcast and sad. She smiled weakly and muttered 'good' before smiling at mum.

"Sorry, I didn't catch your name," said Graham, so I introduced myself and mum and completely ignored Simon.

"What's your sports specialism?" said Graham.

What?

"Um. I don't have one," I said. "I mean - I was a really good gymnast years ago when I was young - but I wouldn't say I had a sports specialism now. Why? Are we supposed to have one?"

I looked at Staff B, watching us with amusement from his position in the front seat. Despite the heat, he had a long-sleeved shirt and white gloves. He must be boiling.

"No one needs any speciality. We're planning to work you hard so you get the most out of the week, but you won't have to do anything you don't want to. Please stop worrying."

"Does your angry-looking mate know that?" I asked. "Only he looks ready to waterboard us if we put a foot wrong."

"Don't mention waterboarding," said Staff B, suddenly getting very serious. "Never mention it. We've all been in the army and experienced terrible things. Please - don't mention it."

"OK," I said meekly, looking at mum. "Sorry."

"But in answer to your question - yes, my angry mate does know, and he's not expecting any sporting prowess. And don't worry. His bark is worse than his bite."

"Phew," said Simon. "I don't have any particular sporting prowess. I don't know what I'd say my skills were."

"Fancying old ladies," I said under my breath as Staff A reappeared at the side of the minibus, looking concerned.

"I can't find her," he said.

"No, there's no one else coming," said Staff B. "We're all here. I've just checked the list. Shall we make a move?"

"No - there's someone else coming," said Staff A. "You know - the girl. I mentioned her."

"Of course," said Staff B. "Fucking hell, how could I forget. Find her. I'll stay here." Then he turned back round to face us.

"We're just waiting for another person to arrive," he said. "She's coming on the Manchester flight. She'll be here any minute."

I turned my attention to mum, who'd gone very quiet.

"Everything OK?" I asked.

"Yes, just feeling a bit tired now. I could do with a nap. Travelling is exhausting when you're older."

"Have a little nap now," I suggested, bundling up my jumper and her coat behind her head so she could lean back on the window. I looked up to see Simon smiling at her. He swung his head away when he saw me looking.

Minutes later, Staff A emerged from the airport building with a glamorous brunette, strikingly slim, in white jeans, a white t-shirt with gold high-heeled sandals, and a gorgeous lemon-coloured scarf around her neck. She looked stunning.

I noticed that Staff A was carrying her bag for her. Great. So, my ancient mother had to take hers herself, but old skinny legs was given a helping hand. Immediately, for no reason, I suddenly felt that something was going on between Staff A and the glamorous brunette. Something about how he was talking to her…leaning in so closely and smiling. It was the first time I'd seen him smile since we arrived.

And what was someone so skinny doing on a weight loss retreat in the first place? Why would she need to be here? It didn't add up.

He helped her into the minibus with such tenderness; it was like a scene from Love Story. "Everything OK?" he asked. "Just say if you need anything." Then he stroked her cheek gently and closed the doors.

"Let's go," he said to Staff B.

"I'm Yvonne," said the attractive lady, and we all murmured greetings back to her as she made herself comfortable, taking up about 1 inch of space.

"Have you known Staff A long," I said.

"No, I've never met him before," she said.

"Oh, you two seemed so close. I assumed you were old friends."

"Nope, we've never met," Staff A added quickly, shouting over from his position in the front seat. "Now make sure you all do up your seatbelts."

"She clicked hers around her and smiled at me, putting out a delicate hand for me to shake. I struggled to get the seat belt done up; it simply wouldn't go around me, so I abandoned it and put my hand out to shake hers. In horror, I realised that my hand was about four times the size of hers. Her tiny, delicate little pink nails looked like those of a child next to my hands which look like shovels.

God, life was so depressing. I think my hands were bigger than hers when I was born. Hands and feet are not supposed to be big if you're a woman.

I long to be delicate, small and adorable at times like these. Or, if the truth be known, I'd settle for being more attractive than my mother. That shouldn't be too much for a woman to ask for, right?

The journey to the villas we were staying in for the retreat took around an hour and a half in boiling sunshine. There was air-conditioning in the vehicle, but it was certainly nothing like strong enough to prevent us from feeling weak with the heat.

"Is there any chance you could turn the air-conditioning up a bit?" I asked.

"You're going to have to get used to this heat, lady; you're going to be exercising in this all day, every day, for the rest of the week," said Staff A.

God, how I wanted to punch him.

"She's right, though; it is hot, is there anything you can do?" said Yvonne.

"Let me have a look," he said. He fiddled with the dials at the front, and when he couldn't make the air-conditioning any colder, he handed her his notebook and advised her to fan herself. I looked from him to her and back again and felt like the most unimportant, ugly person on Earth.

AFTER BAKING IN THE MINIVAN, we arrived at the health camp (I shall insist on calling it that, even though it's a 'military fitness camp') and stepped out onto a street of pretty chalk-coloured houses. Four red brick houses were in the middle of the row of attractive homes in yellow, soft blue and pink. "There are Villa 1, Villa 2, Villa 3 and Villa 4," said Staff B. "You are all in Villa 3. All food is served in Villa 1, and all classes and walks start from Villa 1. That is the main base of the activities. You are all free to go into any of the villas, but your bedrooms are in Villa 1. The keys to each of the villas are kept under the large stones outside the front doors. Once you've let yourself in, please replace the key so the next person can let themselves in. If you accidentally take the key with you, you'll cause chaos. Also, the bedrooms don't lock, so you won't need a key. You'll find it's quite safe. Understand?"

We all nodded to indicate our understanding, but it wasn't enough for grumpy Staff A.

"What was that?" he asked, turning around.

We all murmured that yes, that was fine.

"When you're asked a question, you respond with 'yes, staff'. OK?"

"Yes, staff," we all said.

"You understand that you mustn't move the key from under the rock?"

"Yes, staff," we all said.

"OK then, let's go."

It was a beautiful place, tranquil and with these lovely bright orange and red flowers popping out all over the place

- in baskets outside the villa and even from between the cracks in the wall.

"Come to Villa 1 at 5 pm," said Staff B. "We'll run through the programme for the rest of the week and then go for a quick walk before dinner. OK?"

"Yes, staff," we all replied as I bounced my case and mum's bag down the old stone steps towards the villa's front door. I noticed that Yvonne had gone off with Staff A and Staff B. There was something fishy going on there.

WALKING AND FAINTING

*A*fter the drama of the soldiers frog-marching us to the minibus and the shock of discovering that my mother is way more fanciable than I am, it was a relief to open the door to the villa and find it was gorgeous inside...really lovely. There was a central seating area with three large sofas around a television, a large balcony with a table and chairs, and a good-sized kitchen complete with a washing machine.

The room that mum and I were sharing was downstairs, so I lugged the two bags down the 12 steps and pushed open the door to the room.

When I looked inside, I gasped with relief. I was half expecting bunk beds, camouflage-patterned duvet covers, khaki towels, and no running water, but it was like a lovely hotel room. The best thing was the floor-to-ceiling glass doors that swept open onto a patio with a swimming pool beyond.

"Oh my," said mum. "This looks lovely."

We dumped our bags on the beds and opened the patio

doors before walking to the pool, where Simon and Graham were standing, staring into the water.

Karen walked over to join us. She had very short dark hair cut like a man's hair and quite big features. She wasn't unattractive, just not 'pretty', much to my relief.

"Thank God!" she said as she arrived next to us. "I was worried the rooms would be set up like a military dorm after seeing those two nutters who picked us up from the airport."

"Me too," I squealed louder than I meant to. I was just so excited that the room was a proper hotel room and not a terrible army base. I was also pleased that she seemed as disconcerted by the army stuff as I was. I didn't want to be the only person in the camp who didn't know the army ran it.

"I don't think I was made for soldiering," she said. "I'm just not good at being shouted at."

"Gosh, me neither," I said. "I hate it when people shout at me. And look at the size of this arse - I was not built for running around all over the place."

Karen smiled and laughed, and at that moment, an unlikely bond was created between Karen and me, a bond built on a mutual dislike of khaki and mud and a solidarity to avoid all military-related activity at all costs.

She high-fived me, and I smiled warmly. I'd made a friend. Not the sort of friend who'd be with me for a lifetime, but someone who'd help keep me sane over the coming days.

The only downside of chatting away with Karen was that I had left mum at the mercy of Simon. I looked around as she giggled girlishly. Simon looked away as I gave him the death stare I usually save for customers in the DIY centre who move all the plants to the wrong places.

Simon scurried off, and mum came to join me as we sat on the recliners next to the pool and soaked up the remainder of the afternoon's sunshine. It was heaven…blue skies, a glistening pool and a couple of hours to relax.

We'd been told to meet in villa number one at 5 pm, and it was 3 pm now. From there, we would all go for a walk before dinner. It all seemed reassuringly civilised. I had a lovely room, I'd made an excellent friend, and now I was going on a walk before dinner. Perhaps this whole thing would be OK after all?

I drifted off to sleep until mum woke me up at quarter to five. As soon as I opened my eyes, I was starving. The sun was still beating down on me. I needed a giant gin and tonic and a very large burger and fries.

"Are we eating before going on the walk?" I asked.

"I don't think so," she replied. She'd changed into the gym gear we bought in Sports Direct and looked like she was about to race in the Olympic 100m event.

I staggered out of the sunshine and into the calm haven of my room. I hadn't unpacked and really couldn't be bothered to.

"Do you think I'll be OK in these sandals?" I asked mum. "I can't be bothered to unpack my whole case to get my trainers out."

"Well, obviously trainers would be better," she responded, "but it's only a light evening walk, so I'm sure you'll be fine in those on the first night."

So we headed upstairs in the villa, then strode up the stone steps onto the main road and headed down to villa one.

The main villa was very similar in layout to ours, but a little bit bigger and a bit more bedraggled, if the truth be known. Perhaps it was because so many people sat on the sofas in that villa. After all, it was where everyone congregated, meaning everything looked more worn and tired. In our villa, we had lovely, plump cream sofas, whereas here, they were bedraggled orange ones with a range of mismatched scatter cushions. I much preferred our villa. Mum and I hovered on the edge of the main room, peering in, unsure whether we should enter.

"Come in, come in," said a skinny, very fit-looking woman emerging from a side room: you must be from the Two Fat Ladies blog. I'm Abigail."

"Yes, I'm from Two Fat Ladies. I'm Mary," I said. "This is my mum."

"Hello there, nice to meet you," she said. "I hope you enjoy yourself over the next few days. I'm sure you'll get a lot out of it." Then she glanced at mum: "You're not fat at all. You look great," she said.

"Thank you, how kind," said mum, blushing.

I know Abi's right, mum does look great, but it still felt like a dagger through me that I was as fat as she expected, but mum wasn't.

After the pleasantries (or 'unpleasantries' in my case), we all went for what they laughing called an evening stroll. Trades Descriptions Act, anyone? My idea of an evening stroll is a gentle, enjoyable walk at a sensible pace.

Their idea of an evening stroll is trying to break some imaginary world record, even if it means killing everyone in the group. I tried to keep up, I really did, but the combined forces of strappy sandals, gross unfitness and a body which is twice as large as it should be, prevented me from finishing anywhere near the others. I was about 20 minutes behind them. It was ridiculous, absolutely ridiculous.

"Come on," mum said, in the end, "I could have done the walk five times while you've done it once."

"OK, OK," I said. "Relax. It's day one, no point in wearing yourself out when we've just started. I'm saving myself for later in the week."

The simple truth, of course, was that I was going as fast as possible, and it was the fastest they were likely to see me all week if - indeed - I could tolerate staying all week.

By the time I got back to the villa, I felt more exhausted than I ever have in my life before. I was also wildly starving and thirsty.

"Water?" said Staff B, handing me a beaker. I just nodded at him. I'd completely lost the power of speech.

I was aware that I would be scarlet and soaking wet with sweat - I always was after exercise, but this time I felt much worse than I usually do. I could feel my head spinning, and I kept staggering as I stood there. My knees buckled a bit, but I managed to gain my composure. I'd be fine in a minute. I sipped on the water and waited to feel whole again.

"Are you sure you're OK?" asked mum. "You don't look very well."

"Of course I am," I said once my voice had returned and I'd stopped shaking.

"You're bright red, you know."

"Yes, I do that when I'm tired," I said. "I'm feeling much better now."

As I spoke, I felt everything spin. I felt all unsteady. I heard mum's shout, but it all sounded so far away, I remembered grabbing hold of something that fell to the ground, making a massive sound, and I remember trying to apologise as I hit the deck. I don't remember anything else.

AN INCIDENT WITH DONALD

"**S**he's moving.... she's opening her eyes..."

I could hear mum's voice floating above me, "Can you hear me, love?" she was saying. "Clap if you can hear me."

I moved my hands in a clapping motion and made the tiniest sound - the most pathetic sound in the history of clapping. There was a great cheer, and everyone in the room started clapping too. I looked up to see them all looking down at me, applauding my attempt at a clap, their faces full of pride at my achievement. I felt like a toddler who'd used the potty for the first time.

"Are you feeling alright," said a familiar voice.

"Um, yes, I think," I said vaguely. "Is that you, mum?"

"Yes, darling, it's me," she said.

"Where am I?" I couldn't work out where on earth I was. The people looking down at me looked familiar but weren't my friends. Who were they? Why were they here, in my bedroom?

"You're at the weight loss camp, remember?" said mum.

"We went for a long walk earlier, and you couldn't keep up, then you came back and just fell to the ground."

"Oh God, yes. The weight loss camp. Oh, God. I wish I hadn't asked."

"We're all about to have supper. Perhaps it'll help if we get some food inside you...what do you think?" said a male voice before Staff B's face loomed into view. He smiled at me, and given his position above me, looking down at me, all I could think of was sex. He looked particularly gorgeous from that angle. I knew I needed to move before I pulled him down on top of me and started dry-humping him.

"Food sounds like a good idea," I said, sitting up and looking at the faces around me. They all seemed so concerned.

"Come and sit down," said Karen. "See if you feel better after dinner."

I was helped to my feet by the two 'staffs' and led to the end of the wooden table. The others came over to join me.

"Sit here," Staff B said, pulling out a wooden chair with his gloved hand (still wearing gloves? Very odd) and seating me.

"I'll bring out the food now. Does everyone else want to sit down as well," said Abigail, wiggling her way into the kitchen, giving us all a sight of her peachy derriere clad in expensive lycra.

I continued to sip the beaker of water and smiled as a bowl was laid before me. I peered inside it and looked at mum. She was nodding at me with a look of victory on her face. The bowl contained orange liquid. She was right. We'd been here just a few hours, and already they were serving us bloody carrots.

. . .

DINNER DIDN'T TAKE TOO LONG, as you can probably imagine. Boiled, mashed carrots don't demand a lot of chewing. I finished and waited patiently for something else...anything else - even a celery stick or an apple would have been nice - you know - something to chew on, get my teeth into. But that was it. Just a bowl full of carroty baby food.

"That was quite filling, wasn't it?" said Yvonne, helping me to my feet and asking whether I was OK.

She led me over to the orange sofas and sat me down gently. Everyone else had sat down too. There were about 20 of us on the course, five in each villa. There were people of all shapes and sizes but none as shapely as me. They all seemed very kind and genuinely concerned about me, which was nice; even Simon, the mother-stalker, handed me a cushion and asked whether I needed anything.

I sat back on the sofa and felt quite relaxed. It had been a dramatic start to the trip, but the people were all nice, the accommodation was lovely, and if I ate like that, I'd lose about 40 stone by the end of the week, so it wasn't all bad.

"Shall we play a game," said a guy with ginger hair and a somewhat unflattering ginger goatee beard. I didn't know the guy at all. I knew his name was Mark because he'd introduced himself to me on the walk earlier, but he wasn't in our villa, so I knew nothing about him. I liked him, though. He had been kind enough to offer to stay back and keep me company on the walk earlier while the others had stormed ahead like they were heading into battle.

"Yes, a game sounds good," I replied, more because I thought he was a nice guy, so I wanted to support him than because I have any interest in playing games.

"Yes," said another guy I didn't know. "If no eating or drinking is allowed this evening, a game would be a good distraction."

"OK," said Mark. "I'm going to pose a question; then we

have to go around the room and all answer it. It'll help us to get to know one another as well. Make sure you say your name before you answer."

I was slightly concerned about this - not for my sake - I'm pretty outgoing and happy to answer any questions, but mum's so reserved - I knew she wouldn't want to answer any personal questions.

"What's your weirdest memory of school?" asked Mark.

Fast as lightning, mum's hand shot up.

"I remember a teacher at school being sacked once," she said, laughing as she spoke. "It was so strange...there was an eagle's nest outside, and all the children had to go and look at it on Fridays. For some reason, it always fell to this particular teacher to take us, and she got completely fed up, so one afternoon, when she thought everyone had left the building, she picked up some rocks and hurled them at the nest. It was alarming. I think they were endangered at the time. The birds squawked. The caretaker came, and Mrs Thatchmaker was escorted from the building. No one saw her again, nor the eagles. I don't know whether she killed or terrified them so much that the mummy eagle decided to move them somewhere safer."

I was flabbergasted. Where had mum suddenly got all this confidence from?

"That's so funny. You're a gifted storyteller," said Simon, smiling at mum until he saw me watching him closely and turned away. I swear, if I haven't strangled him by the end of this holiday, it will be a bloody miracle.

"How about you, Simon? Do you have a story from your school days?" I asked, hoping to catch him out without a tale to tell.

"Well, I have a rather vivid and disconcerting memory that I could share with you," he said.

"Do go on," said Yvonne.

"In junior school, our English teacher would put on a new coat of lipstick in the brightest red colour and kiss the boys whenever they misbehaved in class," he said. "Once she'd kissed one of us, we weren't allowed to wipe it off. It happened to me, and it was mortifying...I never crossed her again."

"That's rather a good idea," said mum. "Disciplining the boys without resorting to violence. I like that. I might adopt that if anyone crosses me. I'll kiss them on the cheek, and that will stop them."

"Now I want to cross you," said Simon, smiling lasciviously at mum, causing everyone in the room to look slightly awkward.

"Right; on that note, I'm going to head off to bed. Are you coming, mum?"

"Oh. I might stay here for a while and play this game," she said. "Why don't you stay and join in?"

"I just need to get some sleep," I said, though - in truth - I had a little snack secreted in my bag and needed to eat it before I died of hunger.

"I'll come and walk you back," said mum.

"No, no - you stay. I'll be fine. It takes about 10 seconds to get back. I'll see you later."

"See you in the morning," said Karen, offering a friendly wave.

"I'll walk out with you - I'm heading out," said Yvonne, leaning over to help me to my feet.

"Where are you going?" I asked, hoping she was heading out to the pub. If she was going to a pub, I was going with her. I needed a drink; I wanted to do an 'Aunty Susan', and drink and eat my way through the evening.

"I've found a lovely hotel on the seafront with a great gym, sauna, and spa. I'm going to do a quick workout and sit in the sauna before bed."

"Really?" I said. It baffled me that anyone would want to do extra exercise. "Don't overdo it, though - we've got loads on tomorrow without you trying to squeeze in any extra voluntary stuff tonight."

"I won't overdo it," she said. "See you later."

She walked away in shorts so tight her gynaecologist must have stitched them onto her.

I loitered near the door for a minute, listening to mum and the others still telling their stories. "Come on, a few more silly tales," mum was saying. "I'm enjoying this. I remember something my husband told me. It's a very funny story; he was in his science class, and the teacher was introducing them to the subject of electricity. The teacher told the whole class to hold hands, with the children on the end holding a generator. He would give them a little tingle of electricity and demonstrate how humans conducted it as it went all along the line of children. But the teacher had it turned up too high, and he electrocuted half of them. Your father was hospitalised for a week and had terrible burns on his hands."

"Oh, my goodness," said Staff B, joining the group. "Did that happen to you?"

"No, my husband," said mum.

He looked over at me. "How are you feeling now?"

"OK," I said. "I was just leaving. I feel drained."

"You should get an early night. If you're not feeling right tomorrow, I'll call a doctor, and we'll get him to take a look at you."

"OK," I said. "I'm sure I'll be fine; I just overdid it."

"All the more reason to get an early night then," said Staff B. "Do you want me to walk with you?"

"No, I'll be fine," I said. "Karen, would you mind making sure mum gets back safely?"

"Of course," she said. "No problem at all."

41

"Thank you. Good night everyone," I said, heading through the door as they resumed their game and told silly stories about their time at school. It was only a few steps back to the villa - I walked up the stone steps, through the gate, along to the next villa, down the steps and took the key from under the stone; I let myself in and walked down to the bedroom. It had seemed odd that the rooms didn't lock when I first arrived, but now it was a Godsend - I just pushed the door open, wandered inside and slumped onto the bed. I couldn't be bothered to unpack my suitcase and find my nightie, so I just stripped off, dumped my phone on the bedside cabinet and climbed between the sheets. I fell fast asleep as soon as my head touched the pillow.

AND, to be fair, that's precisely where I would have stayed had it not been for the feel of someone getting into the bed next to me and jumping back out again.

"Who the hell are you?" said a male voice.

I hastily pushed the light on, and there stood a man in his 60s in his Y-fronts. I recognised him from earlier but didn't know his name. I certainly hadn't invited him to join me.

"Get out of my room," I screamed, wrapping the duvet around me as I sat up. "Get out."

"This is my room," said the man.

"This is not your room. It's my room. I share it with my mum."

"Look around," he said. "I've got all my stuff here...see.... You're welcome to stay, but it's not your room."

He was right. His things were laid out on the dressing table; his trainers were neatly by the long mirror. There was no sign of my unpacked suitcase anywhere. Nor any sign of mum.

"Oh shit," I said, wrapping his sheet around me and gathering my clothes. "I don't know how this happened."

"This is villa two," he said. He was staring at my body, not looking at my face, while I spoke to him.

"Oh God, I'm villa three," I said. "I'll be off now."

"No, stay," he said. "Why don't you stay here? I can look after you. I'm Donald, by the way."

"Err, no thanks. I'm going," I said, running from the room, up the stairs and into the right room in the villa. Thankfully mum wasn't back yet, so I climbed into the right bed and fell asleep.

Jesus Christ, Mary, great start to the trip.

SWING YOUR ARMS, MARY

*T*he alarm clock burst into life at 5.30 am, and mum leapt out of bed like a wild salmon. "Come on, up you get," she said. "Remember, we've got our walk this morning before breakfast."

"A walk? You're joking. Were you not there for that walk last night? It was a travesty. We must've done about 20 miles. It almost killed me. Perhaps I shouldn't come this morning?"

"Gosh, you do exaggerate; you'll be fine; just remember to wear your trainers and drink lots of water," said mum pulling back the floor-to-ceiling curtains and letting a most unwelcome flash of early morning light into the room. The pool in the courtyard was glittering in the morning sunshine just outside the patio doors.

"Oh my God - I've just remembered something," I said, staring at the pool. "Last night...something peculiar happened."

"What?" asked mum. "When I got in, you were fast asleep."

"Yes - before that. Oh, God."

Mum was looking at me intently, but I couldn't find the words to explain.

"What happened?" she asked, all wide-eyed, dressed in nothing but her sports bra and an offensively large pair of pants.

"I fainted," I said, "I just remembered that I fainted."

She didn't need to know that I'd jumped into the bed of a 60-year-old called Donald.

"Yes, you did," she said kindly. "Are you feeling OK now?"

"Much better," I said.

I clambered out of bed and started to look around for my phone. I couldn't see it anywhere. I got that horrible lurching feeling in the pit of my stomach that appeared whenever I couldn't find my phone.

"Shit."

I tipped out the contents of my handbag and wracked my brain.

"What on earth's the matter?" asked mum. "What have you lost?"

"My phone. I don't know what I've done with it."

"You probably left it in villa one last night. Let's check when we get there. Or maybe it fell out of your pocket when you fainted?"

"Yes, probably," I said. "Maybe I should look for my phone instead of the walk? I could catch up with you all later?"

"No, you're coming on the walk," said mum. "We've come all this way to get fit and healthy…this is a great chance for you to lose some weight and start to feel good. It's silly to start missing out on things on day one."

"OK, OK," I said. "I'll come on the walk, but you have to be aware that if it's anything like last night's walk, it will kill me, and there's every chance you'll be arrested for murder for making me go on it."

"The walk last night was about five miles, that's all, and it was very nice. All the people we met were lovely, and the scenery was spectacular. Come on, up you get. We're walking along the beach this morning; hopefully, we'll have time to come back and jump in that pool afterwards. Doesn't it look spectacular? Just spectacular."

"I knew it was a mistake bringing you," I said as I staggered like a drunk into the bathroom. Why couldn't my mum be miserable in the mornings like everyone else on earth? As I clambered into the shower, I could hear her singing to herself as she got changed. God, the backs of my legs were aching. The truth was that I was so bloody unfit that every bit of exercise we did would render me exhausted and in pain.

On the other hand, Mum was a regular walker, played a bit of tennis, and did a lot of gardening. In short, she was about 30 years older than me but twice as fit as me. And if that wasn't an embarrassing prospect, I thought to myself as I washed my hair and clambered out of the shower; I didn't know what was.

I followed mum out of the room, my hair was still wet, and my unforgiving gym kit made me feel the size of a house. We walked to villa one, where we were all meeting. I shuffled along in a sulk, staring at the ground while mum strode ahead and shouted 'morning' to everyone she encountered. I decided I was not saying good morning to anyone.

"Mary, Mary," came a shout from a man running towards us. I gasped when I saw him. It was Donald - the guy from last night...the guy who had come into his room and caught me in fast-asleep in his bed. Oh, God. In his hand, he held my phone.

"You left this in my room," he said. I looked at him aghast, alarm spreading across my face like an uncontrollable rash.

He mistook my alarm for confusion. "When you were in my bed last night. Remember? Well, you left this behind."

I looked at mum, who was open-mouthed.

"It's not how it looks," I mouthed. "I went into his bed by mistake."

Mum's mouth was still wide open.

"IT WAS A MISTAKE."

"I'll say it was," she said. "Having an affair with an older man on holiday when you have such a lovely boyfriend at home…a huge mistake."

"Mum, I didn't have an affair. I went to the wrong villa, that's all. They all look the same; the doors aren't locked. It was an easy mistake to make."

Mum looked at me and shook her head. "You're going to ruin it with Ted, aren't you? He's such a lovely, perfect man. You must be nuts."

"Ted is lovely, but he's far from perfect."

Mum sighed and looked very disappointed. In front of us saw Staff B, warning up by bending over in perilously tight shorts.

"One word of advice, though, Mary. If you accidentally get into a man's bed, get into the bed of a man like Staff B, not dopey Donald, won't you."

"Will do," I said as Staff B stood up. He had on the shortest shorts but still wore a long-sleeved t-shirt and those white gloves he seemed obsessed with. He was stubbly and muscular and oozed masculinity. Mum was right. That would have been a better bed to have found myself in.

"Ready for our little morning walk," he said, giving me a gentle hug. "You don't have to look so sad. It's only a quick stroll along the beach."

"I'm not sad," I said. "I don't believe you. It won't be a quick walk at all: I'm wise to your madness now. I'm well aware that when you say a quick walk along the beach, you mean that we're going to do an Ironman triathlon in world record-beating time."

"Not quite," he said with a warm laugh. "It's just a morning stroll to knock away the cobwebs."

He grinned as he walked away, but I knew he was lying. 'Stroll'? Really? I didn't think it would be at all stroll-ish.

I sat on the small stone wall outside the villa while everyone else warmed up. I knew I should join in, but I felt so self-conscious, so I sat and focused on the lovely purple flowers growing out of the rocks next to us, gently cupping one of them in my hand and making a mental note to find out what they were, they were so beautiful - like tiny pansies with lovely, open faces. I looked up to see Donald watching me, and I blushed as I looked away. How could I have been so bloody stupid?

Everyone else was ready to go, some jogging on the spot and waving their arms around, some starting to stretch their calves out like they were bloody Paula Radcliffe or something. Then it was time to leave...

We all walked down the street quite fast. Much faster than I would've chosen to do had I been walking by myself, I had to do little skippy steps to keep up with them. We then went down the steps leading to the beach. "Come on, let's get a bit of speed up, shall we," said Staff B, jogging down them, then sprinting across the sand. Oh, Christ. I just wasn't fit enough to do any of this; as I ran down the steps, I could feel my boobs bouncing up and down and my stomach moving like it had a mind of its own. Instinctively I pulled my t-shirt down and held it flat against my body as if to disguise the horrible flesh beneath it. I hated being fat. Being fat was awful.

"What's up with you?" said Staff B. "You look like you're fed up. Look at your mum; she's jogging along the beach."

"You said it would be a walk," I bit back.

I looked up to see mum running along with the others. They lifted their knees as high as possible and had their arms out in front of them so that their knees were tapping against their hands. They were already miles in front.

"I can't do any of this because I'm too fat," I said disconsolately. "It hurts when I run and skip and jump."

"Well, walk then. The important thing is to keep moving."

"I'm not going to lose all this weight by walking, am I?" I said.

"Yes, of course, you will. If you vow to move whenever you can, however, you want, you'll lose the weight. It's not rocket science."

"But it will take years of effort, and I haven't got the motivation for it."

"You don't need motivation. Stop thinking of exercising as some horrible punishment. Look, this is how I see it. First thing - speed up a little bit and walk next to me. That's not too bad. Walking at this speed where you can feel yourself getting out of breath will use many more calories."

"OK, I can do that," I said.

"Now, swing your arms as you walk," he said. I swung them by my side. "See how fast you can swing them," he said. I swung them backwards and forwards as quickly as possible and noticed that my pace was speeding up.

"A little tip for you there, Mary," he said. "You will find that your legs will go as fast as your arms are swinging, so if you want to make yourself go faster, swing your arms faster, and your legs will keep up. If you walk along like you have been doing with your arms hardly swinging, you will automatically walk more slowly."

"Good tip," I said.

"And you know what you've just been saying about losing weight?"

"Yes," I said, hoping he would give me some magical

formula for losing weight that would enable me to shift ten stone this week.

"I think you need to stop thinking about it as being all about weight loss. Yes, you want to lose weight, but you want weight loss to be the by-product of what you do to get yourself feeling fit, healthy and fabulous.

"I think you need to focus on looking after yourself a bit more. So, don't put anything in your mouth that isn't going to do you good. Drink lots of water because it will stop headaches and make you feel full of energy, and use your legs and your body as much as possible because being fit is the key to feeling great.

"All you are doing from now onwards is looking after yourself and trying to feel as great as possible.

"Stop trying to tick off the number of pounds you've lost, and stop mentally totting up how many months it will be before you meet some arbitrary desired weight. Just take each day as it comes and, on that day, do everything you can to make yourself feel and look better. How about that as a plan?"

The arm swinging seemed to work well, and I had almost caught up with the rest of the group, who were busy doing star jumps on the beach near the cliff.

"Okay, I can do that," I said. "Thank you."

He leaned in, gave me a big hug, and said: "You know, Mary Brown, it's all going to be okay. You're young, attractive, and prepared to do something to make yourself fitter and healthier. You've got a beautiful life ahead of you - you've just got to believe that."

"I believe," I said in a loud, mock American accent, being sarcastic with him as he smiled and walked away, but the truth was that I did feel quite good, better than I had for ages, and I did feel as if I believed I could do something about the way I looked. I smiled at his retreating back and thought. "This could be the best week of my life."

Then I saw Donald approaching, clutching a small purple flower like the ones I'd admired earlier. "Hello, bedmate," he said with an unattractive wink. "Thought you might like this…."

WEIGHTS AND MEASURES

"*R*ight, let's get going with the weighing and measuring," said Staff A, clapping his hands and rubbing them together. "We want to make sure that you know exactly where you are beginning of the course so you can see how much you progress in just a few days."

This struck me as odd. Hadn't Staff B just spent 10 minutes having an emotional chat with me on the beach where he said I shouldn't focus on weight?"

I couldn't resist mentioning this...in the hope that they would abandon their plans to weigh us.

"Yes, Mary, that's true," he said, a hint of exasperation sneaking into the corners of his voice. "But this is to help you see what impact we can have when we work hard. It's a motivational tool more than anything else. Does that make sense?"

"Yes," I said. Though it didn't. I didn't understand why a course which decried the process of weighing and measuring weighed and measured us all at the beginning and the end of the course.

I think he could sense that I was still very confused. "OK,

I can see that it seems odd," he said. "I wouldn't advise worrying too much about your weight; look at how you look and how you feel and what makes you happy rather than what random numbers on a scale tell you.

"We are all different builds, all different makeups; the idea that everybody who is 5'6" should weigh the same is wrong, but it's a useful guide to see how you've changed over the course."

I nodded at him, realising that I wouldn't get out of this and they would measure me regardless. I suppose the weighing gives them a handy marketing tool: 'lose half a stone in four days' is a lot more exciting a proposition than 'get a bit healthier, but not measurably so because we don't believe in measuring and weighing.'

I was first up. That would teach me to answer back to the instructor. I stepped onto the scales and watched the numbers in front of me rising with astounding speed, getting bigger and bigger until they settled on... 15 stone and 2 pounds.

"That's wrong!" I squealed, jumping off as if the thing had bitten me. I saw the looks of horror on those waiting in the dining room for their turn to be measured. A bit like that time when I screamed in the dentist's at such a blood-curdling volume that the waiting room had cleared by the time I came out.

"I can't possibly be that heavy. That's the weight a baby elephant should be, or a car or something, not a human being."

"Don't worry about it," Staff A said. "It's just a number. It just tells you where you are now, and then we can see where you are at the end of the week and work out what changes have taken place."

"But to be over 15 stone...that's insane," I said. "Your scales are drunk."

"Fifteen stone!" squealed mum. "That can't be right, can it?"

"No!" I shouted back. "It most certainly isn't."

"You told me you were 13 stone."

"I am," I said. "The scales are wrong."

I looked at Staff A. "The scales are right, aren't they?" I said miserably.

"Yep," he said. "But try not to worry. You're in the right place with the right people. I will help you sort all this out. OK?"

"Yes," I said.

I walked back to mum.

"That can't be right," she said.

"No," I said, shaking my head vigorously.

"So, the scales were wrong?" she asked.

"Yes," I said. "They hadn't set them up properly."

"So, how heavy are you?" asked mum.

"Thirteen stone," I replied.

Mum went on next and came skipping back to declare that she was ten and a half stone. "I'm pleased because I thought my weight was creeping up towards 11 stone."

"Yes, that would have been awful," I said uncharitably while I chewed on the fact that mum was so much lighter than me.

It took a little while for the whole weighing process to happen, so we were treated to a film to keep us entertained while they did it. Not a film in the way you or I might recognise it - no Sex & The City or Bridesmaids or anything, just a film about being healthy and getting fit. And no popcorn, of course. Not even the naff plain stuff that I accidentally buy sometimes by mistake when I'm aiming for the toffee-coated stuff.

Staff B stepped up to sort out the video. After a considerable amount of trouble connecting his laptop to the large screen, including showing everyone all his emails, he appeared to have asserted some technological control.

"Phew," he said. "That was harder than I thought it would be. OK. Before we start on today's sessions, we have a quick video to show you while the weighing is going on. Before I do that, a quick question - who was alarmed by their weight and is disappointed at weighing more than they thought they would?"

Loads of hands shot up, including bone-skinny Yvonne's, which annoyed me. I bet her weight hardly registered on the scale.

"Well, I want you to stop worrying - the reason for us weighing you is to show you that if you eat right and exercise well, you WILL lose weight. But we'd very much like you to park the whole weight issue.

"As staff explained to Mary earlier, we mustn't emphasise how much we weigh. What's important is how you feel, and to most of you, it'll be how you look. I'm sure you'd much rather look great in a dress than hit a particular weight measurement but not look great. Isn't that right?"

"Yes," we all chorused.

"And how are you all feeling today?"

"Fat!" I shouted while everyone else shouted, "great."

THE VIDEO SHIMMERED INTO LIFE, and a rather sombre-looking guy dressed in a white coat like a doctor or scientist appeared on the screen.

"Obesity is such a problem that we spend more on it than on the fire service, the police service and the judiciary all put together," he said.

Sighs of disbelief drifted in from all corners of the room.

"It's alarming, isn't it?" he continued. "It shows what a

problem it is. And it also shows how hard it is to deal with - do you know why that is? Why don't we all eat less?

"The reason is in our biology - we are forcing ourselves to live a life that suits our minds, not our bodies. We have bodies designed to store food and a brain designed to be attracted to food - these are survival instincts that worked when food was scarce. But now we're living in a part of the world where there's plenty of food while these instincts remain.

"So - what you're all wondering is - what do we do about it? These facts might help give you a clue: we are now 20% less active than we were in the 1960s. Exercise is a vital part of good health."

There were mumblings of agreement, and I mumbled along with them but to be honest, I don't think exercise is the key to anything but abject misery.

"Exercise is one of five things you need to do to lose weight. Numerous investigations have shown this. These are the five things: eat less, exercise more, drink water when you're hungry, remember that your body was designed for times when there was no food around, and it had to conserve everything you put into it carefully, and – finally - walk, walk and walk again."

I was starting to get frustrated with the whole thing. If I could 'eat less', I wouldn't be obese in the first place.

"There are lots of diets being promoted all the time," science man continued. "Lots of them are marketed as the answer to all your weight loss problems. But there are real issues associated with opting for the latest fad diet, or the diet that appears to be 'proven' to be the best way to lose weight. Let me demonstrate."

Suddenly science man was standing in front of a university.

"So, a study conducted at this university found that low-carb dieters fared much better than those who followed a low-fat diet and showed better results on blood tests that indicate cardiovascular health.

"Then, a few months later, a University of South Carolina study published in the International Journal of Applied and Basic Nutritional Sciences found the greatest weight loss was found on a high-carbohydrate vegan diet.

So, within two months, the evidence points to the fact that low-carb diets work and high-carb diets work.

"There have been reports that depression and obesity are strongly linked, that eating breakfast helps you lose weight, and then, a few months later, further research to show that none of that is true.

"The reason I'm saying all this is to show you that having a healthy scepticism about studies is important. Some are good, and some are bad. Even the good ones can be overturned with another study a few years on."

The video ended with a montage of good old-fashioned advice about eating a healthy, balanced diet: Don't eat too much, drink lots of water and avoid mood-altering foods like sugar-laden drinks, cakes and coffee that send your hormones into overdrive."

"So, what do you think of that?" said Staff B.

No one spoke, so I thought I ought to.

"Oh, God. It's all so complicated," I said.

"Exactly. The point is that you are unlikely to achieve a good long-term result if you try to do fad diet plans or exercise regimes or try to miss out on one food group to shed the pounds. If you keep it simple and follow our advice - not only will you look better, but you'll all be much healthier. Does that make sense?"

"Yes," I said. It did make sense. I was sick of following stupid diet fads. I would give this a go."

"Good. So, on that note, let me introduce you to today's activities."

He pulled out a blackboard that was full of classes. I swear to God, there were ten on there.

"Are you having a laugh?" I asked more loudly than I intended to.

"You don't have to do all the classes," said Staff A, but you'll get a much better result if you do everything."

"The result will be me in intensive care," I said.

"No one wants that," said the instructor. "Just do whatever you can and try to push yourself as much as possible."

I sensed my constant talking back at him was starting to wear thin. Still, the blackboard. You should have bloody seen it: First was boxing, then circuits, then cycling, followed by swimming, and that was all before lunch. In the afternoon, something called heat, followed by body combat, body conditioning, body pump and Pilates, then more boxing. JESUS CHRIST

"Before all that, though - breakfast," he said.

Possibly the only sensible thing anyone has said since I arrived in this God-forsaken place.

STAFF B COMES TO VISIT

The day was exhausting. I mean - terrifyingly tiring, and I only did half of it. I opted to miss every other class to cope with it. The day was to end with a final boxing class held on the top of a steep hill, which practically took crampons and advanced mountaineering equipment to climb. I sat on the edge of my bed. Would it be so bad if I didn't go? I'd missed the first boxing class in the morning, but in my defence, I had been to more classes that day than I'd been in the previous year, and there were two more days to go. Surely I could miss this one out?

Under the pretence of looking for my water bottle, I told mum to go ahead and I'd join her.

"OK," she said, smiling and dancing out of the room. Honestly, she's indefatigable.

As soon as she had gone, I flopped onto the bed and experienced utter joy and exhilaration, lying there, eyes closed, with the sun warming me through the patio windows. Without moving from my position on the bed, I eased off my trainers, pushing down the back of the heel with my other foot, and hearing the gentle plop as it hit the floor. I did the same with the other trainer and lay back about as comfortable as any woman has ever been in her life before.

As I slinked into the bed and dropped off to sleep, I heard a gentle knock at the door. It must be mum. She must've realised that I wasn't coming and had come back for me. "I'm too tired for boxing," I shouted. "I'm going to have a little sleep before dinner."

It wasn't mum's voice that replied but a deep male voice. "Can I come in? It's Staff B."

I sat up in the bed, ran my hands through my hair and adjusted my clothing to look as alluring as possible. Well, as alluring as a 15 stone woman can look in lycra when she's been exercising all day. I cursed myself for not having come in and had a shower.

"Of course," I said. I arranged myself as seductively as possible, my head resting against my hand, my arm bent, one leg over the other as I lay on my side, hoping to look feminine and elegant.

"Hello there," he said, walking inside and sitting in the chair beside my bed. "Everything okay?"

"Yes, fine," I said. "I feel completely knackered. I couldn't face boxing. I'm also weak with hunger. I don't cope very well without food."

"Well, that's what I wanted to talk to you about," said Staff B. "You didn't come along for the snack just now before boxing. Everyone else was desperate for it. I figured perhaps you weren't feeling very well?"

"Snack?" I said. "I didn't know there was a snack?"

"Yes." That's when he presented me with a tiny piece of flapjack. Honestly, it was minuscule... about the size of my thumbnail, but nothing has ever given me greater pleasure.

"Is this for me?" I asked as if he had just given me a jumbo jet or something.

"All yours," he said. I picked it up off the plate as if it was the most precious thing ever, and put it onto the end of my tongue, determined to make it last as long as possible.

"I can't believe I missed a snack," I said to Staff B. "I've never missed a snack in my life before."

He smiled warmly.

"Why aren't you with the boxers?" I asked.

"We're mixing things up - Staff A and Abi are taking this one so I can get a couple of hours off. I've got a bit of paperwork to do, and I'm working the session tomorrow and being in charge of the great big martial arts, combat and boxing three-hour marathon session on Thursday morning."

"WHAT?"

"Yep - three hours of boxing, kicking and wrestling. Pure joy"

"Good God, this is hardcore," I said. "Why so much boxing and fighting?"

"It's a military fitness camp. What did you think we'd be doing? Needlework?"

"Ha, ha," I said. "Can I ask you something?"

"Fire away," he said.

"Why are you called Staff B? It seems weird that we can't just call you by your name."

"My name is Martin," he said. "But here, they like the instructors to be called staff."

"Why? It's absurd to insist on everything being so military when we're just flabby people wanting to lose a few pounds."

"Yes," he said with a smile. "But there is a sensible reason. You see – in the army, you don't have a rank when you're a PT instructor; you're all called staff, so no one knows what rank you are. The reason for that is that physical fitness is very important, and you couldn't have a situation where the physical trainer is instructing someone of a higher rank, and the person of the higher rank didn't want to do it, so pulled rank.

"They decided the best thing was that when it came to physical training, everyone involved was called staff and were all equal."

"Oh, I see, "I said. "That makes sense. I can see why they would do that. Why don't they explain that to us? It would make us feel much better about the names we call you."

"I don't know," said Staff B. "Maybe I'll mention it to Abi?"

"Did you like it in the army?" I asked.

"I loved it," he said, taking off his boots, putting his feet up on the bed and removing his watch as he made himself comfortable. Interestingly, the gloves stayed on.

"My dad was a soldier, and my grandad before him. All of the men in my family end up in the army; it's in the blood. It's all I ever wanted to do, and when I got into the army, I felt like I'd come home. Then there was the tour to Afghanistan where it all went wrong."

"What happened?"

"In short, I had my arm blown off," he said bluntly. "It's why I always wear long-sleeved shirts. Look…" He lifted his shirt sleeve, and I saw the prosthetic arm beneath it. I'd never noticed before. He always wore gloves and always wore long sleeves, and no one was anyone the wiser.

"Gosh. Did someone shoot at you? What happened?"

"No, it was a landmine. It was in an area where we knew there were landmines, but I was much further out than we thought they went. Four of us were standing there. One guy died."

"Oh, God. I'm so sorry," I said. "How awful"

"Yep," he said, nodding. "All pretty awful. When I left, I had no idea what I'd do with myself. As I explained - being a soldier was in my blood...I couldn't think how I'd survive without it. Doing military-style training for civilians saved me. I couldn't have gone into an office job or anything; it would have driven me nuts. Or worked in a shop. Can you imagine that? Working in a shop all day…."

"I work in a shop," I said timidly.

"Oh. Sorry," he replied. "I just think it would have driven me insane."

"Don't worry. It drives me insane sometimes," I said. "What about Staff A? Was it the same sort of thing with him? Injured abroad."

Staff B moved to stand up. "No, it was very different with him. I better head off. I'll see you at dinner." With that, he was gone; he had deliberately refused to talk about why Staff A had left the army. I knew, instinctively, that there was something odd about this. Staff B's reaction triggered a little spark of interest in me. Right. That would be my mission. To find out why the guy had left the army and why he had such a close relationship with skinny Yvonne.

It wasn't long before mum came back from boxing looking so bedraggled and exhausted that I was doubly pleased I hadn't gone on the trip up the hill. "What happened to you?" she said, falling onto her bed like a rag doll. "You missed the snack and everything."

"Yes, sorry," I said.

"What's this?" Mum held up Staff B's watch that he'd left on the edge of her bed.

"Oh yes - that's Staff B's," I said, not quite realising how dodgy that sounded.

She handed me the watch; her eyebrows raised so high they had disappeared into her hairline. "Staff B's," she said. "You know I wasn't serious when I said you should try to bed him next time. You know I was only joking, don't you?"

"Ha ha ha," I said. "You're so funny, mum. Nothing happened. He just came to see me."

"And undressed?"

"No, he didn't undress. He just took his watch off."

"Yep - very likely story," said mum. "Very likely story indeed."

"He dropped my snack off if you must know. And he wanted to see how I was. I guess he thought it was so unlikely that I would miss the chance of food that he thought something was wrong with me."

"So, let's summarise things so far - on the first night here, you end up in Donald's bedroom, and on the second night here, Staff B ends up in your bedroom. You're having a good trip so far, aren't you?"

Mum laughed as she said it, and I just shook my head and lay back down on the pillow. There was no point in defending myself when she was in such a silly mood.

"I think all the exercise is making you high," I said. "You're behaving like a drunk teenager. And actually, he told me about his time in the army and how he had to leave because his arm was blown off."

"Blown off?"

"Yep. I've got your attention now, haven't I? A landmine blew his arm off, so he left. He has an artificial arm."

"Gosh, I've never noticed that before."

"No, but you remember how he always wears long sleeves and gloves? That's why."

"I want to hear more about this," said mum. "I'll have a shower after dinner instead of now. What else did he say?"

"Not much, to be honest. He said that when he left, he didn't know what he'd do with himself...all his family are soldiers, and it's all he ever wanted to do. I think this place saved him."

"Gosh, that's incredible. Fancy losing your arm."

Mum wandered towards the patio windows and looked at the pool as she spoke.

"Makes you realise how grateful you should be, doesn't it?" she said.

. . .

WE WALKED UP to dinner together, both of us fantasising about the food that might be on offer. Mum thought it might be a gorgeous Italian meal, a lovely pasta dish with fresh lobster and freshly caught prawns. I said it would probably be a big steak and chips or maybe a massive American burger with chips covered in chilli con carne.

"Shall we have a big bowl of nachos to start?" Mum said.

"Oh yes," I agreed. "And some of those salt and pepper calamari that are delicious. Maybe we should have a big selection of starters before we get onto our main course."

"Good idea," said mum.

We got into the dining room, salivating with excitement at the thought of the food we had been discussing, then sat down and winced a little as they brought out a bowl of broccoli soup.

"At least it's not carrot," said Mum.

"Oh yes, it is," said Abi, appearing beside us. "It's broccoli and carrot."

"Oh good," I said. "Exactly what we were both hoping for."

As soon as dinner was over, I wanted to return to the room... I had visions of falling into an early sleep. Some guys talked about going for a walk, but that felt like massive self-abuse. Why would you do more exercise? It baffled me.

"What are you up to tonight?" I asked Yvonne, who was sitting opposite me.

"I'm going to head off to the sauna again," she said, standing up and moving to leave the table.

"Do you mind if I come with you?" said Simon, standing up as well.

I was intrigued as to how this would all pan out. If Yvonne was genuinely going to the gym and sauna and not just using it as an excuse to escape and see Staff A, she'd have no problem with Simon going along with her. I glanced at mum, and we both eagerly awaited Yvonne's reply.

"Not this time Simon," said Yvonne. She smiled at him and left the room at top speed. Minutes later, I was chatting to mum, sitting just across from Staff A, when he jumped up.

"Right - I need to get off," he said. "See you all tomorrow."

With that, he left, and I turned to mum.

"Right, that's it. Something's going on. Tomorrow night we're going to follow him," I said.

"Oooo...that does sound exciting," said mum. "But what if he sees us?"

"We'll say we're going for a walk or something. I have to know what he's up to."

It wasn't long after the departure of the star-crossed lovers that the games started.

"I've got a fun game," said Donald, and though I'm usually completely up for late-night games, I do like a few drinks inside me first. The prospect of playing silly 'tell all' games with strangers while completely sober was not appealing.

Also, I was starving, and I know you're going to be cross with me for this, but I had a packet of crisps in my bag from the flight, and I could no longer fight off the urge to eat them. More than anything, I wanted to go back, eat the crisps, shower and relax.

I MADE it back without incident this time, going straight to the right villa. Perhaps the lure of the crisps sent me straight to the right place. I let myself in, rummaged through my bag tucked into the far corner of the wardrobe, and pulled out the crisps and a can of coke. Did I not mention that I had coke as well? Oh well, it's only a small can, hardly worth mentioning.

Then I turned towards the patio doors. It was so hot in the room because mum had turned off the air conditioning when we left. I planned to sit outside in the moonlight and eat the crisps.

But then I saw something amazing...I blinked and checked again. My eyes hadn't mistaken me; there was someone in our pool doing synchronised swimming. It was quite mesmerising. I mean - the lady was really good. She was dressed in a 1950s-style costume and bathing cap and kept bursting out of the water, like they do, kicking her golden legs high into the air while she was upside down. I opened the patio doors and stepped outside, walking as quietly as possible to avoid disturbing her.

She didn't stop. She carried on flinging her legs in the air and shooting upwards out of the water with a nose clip on, hair scraped back into a bun, and sparkly swimming costume, smiling wildly for an imaginary audience. She didn't see me, but I watched her for a while. There was tinny music playing while she performed. She must be a competitive swimmer; she had a proper routine and everything.

"Mary, where are you?" came a voice from behind me. Mum was back. I rushed to the shrub nearby, stuffed my crisps and coke into it, and then ran back towards the villa.

"What are you doing out there?" she asked.

"Come out," I said. "I've just been watching this amazing synchronised swimmer in the pool."

"What?" said mum.

"Come and see," I insisted. "She's really good. She's got a sparkly costume on and everything."

Mum looked at me like I'd gone completely mad, but she followed me outside all the same. When we got there, the swimmer had gone...disappeared into the night with her tape recorder.

I looked at mum and could tell she didn't believe a word I was saying.

"She was here - she had a proper routine and the nose clip and everything, she was really good."

"OK," mum said.

"It's true. She was here."

"Maybe you shouldn't get so much sun tomorrow," she said, turning back inside. I wasn't going anywhere before devouring my crisps. Once mum's back was turned, I rushed over to the shrub and crouched behind it to eat my illicit food. God, it was amazing - it tasted so incredibly flavoursome. Too flavoursome, my lips were tingling, and my head was buzzing.

Then I heard mum's voice again.

"What are you doing now?" she asked.

"I'm just looking at this shrub," I said, tipping the remainder of the crisps into my mouth. Mum had started to walk towards me. There was no way I could finish my mouthful before she got to me.

But I didn't want to be caught with a mouthful of crisps either. And I certainly wasn't going to spit them out. As mum got close, I panicked. I jumped up and threw myself into the pool, fully clothed with so many crisps in my mouth that my face looked like a puffer fish.

"Goodness Mary, I do worry about you," said mum. "I think you should stay out of the sun as much as possible tomorrow."

I nodded and gave as much of a smile as possible without losing the crisps, and mum went back inside. I followed her, soaking wet and having convinced my mother that I was ready to be locked up in a lunatic asylum.

SHE FLOATS LIKE A BUTTERFLY
AND STINGS LIKE A BEE

"*O*K, everyone, did you enjoy your breakfast?" asked Staff A, smiling and waiting for a response. I sat with my arms folded across my chest and looked around the room. We were a wildly disparate group - different ages, sizes, shapes and backgrounds, but I was fairly confident that we had one thing in common: none of us had enjoyed the Dickensian brown slop that had passed for breakfast. Thank God for the family bag of cheese and onion crisps I had eaten behind the shrub last night (yes, it was a family bag - don't judge me).

"OK, no huge votes of approval for breakfast then," Staff A continued, having noticed the lack of his response to his enquiry about our food.

"In its favour: it is healthy and will keep you full, and that's all that matters. Now, let's take a quick look at what we're doing today."

I found myself staring at him as he spoke. He seemed to be directing all his comments to Yvonne. Or was that just my imagination? There was a special bond between them. The question was - what bond? The way he'd acted with her at the airport - like long-lost friends...he seemed fascinated by her, but she had insisted she'd never met him before.

"Right," said Staff A, and he held up a blackboard full of activities for the day, detailing what had been arranged for us on the hour, every hour.

"I know it seems like a lot," he said, second-guessing what we were all thinking. "But I urge you to come to everything. As I keep saying, these few days will change your life, but only if you let them. My advice to you is to go with the flow. Stop stressing about not having as much food as you'd like, and stop worrying about how hard the exercise will be. If you're struggling, stop, but don't not start. The worst thing you can do this week is to sit back and not participate. This week is so short - it'll be gone in no time. If you work hard, you'll lose weight, feel great and have a whole new approach to life."

"That's right," said Staff B, joining 'A' at the front of the room. "I know we keep saying it, but you will get as much out of this week as you allow yourself to. It's day three - in some ways, the hardest day. It's the course's 'hump day'. You'll get tired, you'll get hungry, and you'll feel frustrated, but you'll get through it, and at the end of the week, you'll look back and realise how much you can do if you try your hardest. This will act as inspiration when you get home. Does that make sense to everyone?"

There were murmurs of general agreement because what he said made perfect sense...it all sounded very hard, and I'd rather lie by the pool eating crisps and watching the late-night synchronised swimmer.

THE FIRST CLASS of the day was combat skills. Blimey, they like their boxing here. This was the third class in which we'd been asked to don boxing gloves and hit one another. The third one! Luckily, I'd missed the first two. On what planet do you need to do three boxing classes in two days, for God's sake?

We were told to get into pairs, and I could see Donald approaching me - there was no way I was going with him. Mum immediately skipped over to me, assuming I'd be with her. This was something I wasn't very keen on at all. She's half my size, and I'm half her age. That can't be a fair match-up, surely?

We were given gloves to put on - big, red gloves that you see proper boxers wearing. No part of this seemed OK to me.

"Come on then," said mum, who had been to the two previous boxing classes and thought she knew what she was doing. She danced around like she was Anthony Joshua or something. "Come and get me if you dare," she said.

I held my hands up in the boxing position and copied the stance that Staff B was demonstrating at the front of the class.

"A couple of light punches into your partner's gloves...let's see how you get on," he said.

Mum punched out so ferociously that she sent my hands spinning away from my face.

"Gotcha," she said. Christ, she was tougher than she looked.

I shadow-boxed back, avoiding hitting her with any force because I knew I'd hurt her.

"Come on, you can do better than that," said mum. "Show us what you're made of."

I continued to tap her gloves with mine and tried to ensure my technique was as good as possible rather than putting all my power into the shots.

Staff A wandered over. "Is that all you've got?" he asked. "I'm sure you've got more power than that."

I didn't rise to the bait; I just tapped gently. Then we

swapped over again, and it was mum's turn to hit. She didn't afford me anything like the same kindness. She whacked me ferociously…with every muscle she had. As the punches rained down on me, I swung my arms up to defend myself.

"Now lots of little jabs," said Staff. "Punching as quickly and as hard as you can."

Oh hell. I lifted my arms to protect myself from the onslaught that was bound to come my way. Mum swung at me as I shielded my face from the punches.

When we changed over, I just shadow-boxed back.

"Come on, you can do better than that," said mum. "Come on, show us what you're made of."

What happened to the kindly mother who'd knitted me mittens and made me fish fingers for tea? This was a terrible development.

I continued to tap lightly on her gloves, showing admirable restraint while perfecting the noble art. Staff A charged over to us. He didn't agree that restraint was a good idea. "I'm sure you've got more power than that."

I didn't rise to the bait; I just tapped gently. "Come on, Mary. The harder you hit, the leaner you'll be." I'm not sure whether this statement would stand up to rigorous scientific examination, but I got what he was saying…put more effort in. But the thing is, I didn't want to hit my mum.

When the whistle went, and we swapped over again, it was mum's turn to hit. She whacked me ferociously…Blimey. My hands went flying back, and mum looked delighted with herself. Staff A applauded her.

"That's it," he said. "That's the way to do it."

The whistle went, and we changed over for the final time. I was completely exhausted…punching was hard, but even standing there with your hands up, being punched, was hard work.

"Now then, come on, Mary, you can do it," goaded Staff A,

clapping his hands and urging me to put all my weight behind my punches. I swung out a little more than I had previously, and I don't know whether mum wasn't quite concentrating or had dropped her hands a bit, but my fist flew through and caught her right on her left eye with a tremendous thump.

"Ah," she screamed, falling to the ground, holding her head. It was like it was all taking place in slow motion...mum spinning backwards, raising her hands to protect her face.

"Oh my goodness, what have you done?" said Staff A, rushing to mum's side and glaring at me.

"I just did what you told me to do," I said. "I did what you told me to do when I knew very well that this would happen; I should have trusted my instincts."

I bent down next to mum, who was telling me not to worry, and that everything was fine, but I could see her left eye was already starting to close up and would no doubt go black overnight and leave her looking like she'd been street fighting.

"Let's get you back to the villa," said Staff A, lifting mum gently to her feet and dropping his arm around her shoulder. I gathered mum's stuff and ran after them while the rest of the group stopped and stared at us.

Back at the villa, the chef came out of the kitchen with an ice pack and asked what had happened.

"Mary punched her mum in the face," said Staff A.

"It wasn't quite like that," I said. "We were doing the boxing class, and I just caught mum on the side of the face."

"Oh my goodness, what made you punch her so hard?"

"I was just doing as I was told," I said. "When I wasn't punching hard, I was told to hit harder."

"Yes, but not give your mum a black eye!" said Staff A. "No one told you to injure her."

"Are you OK, mum?" I said.

"Honestly, I'm absolutely fine. Please don't worry." But as she looked up at me, her left eye was weeping and looking swollen; I felt ill to the pit of my stomach.

"You should probably sit this next class out," said Staff A.

"Yes, sure, I think that's a good idea. Thanks," I replied. "I'll go back to my room for a lie-down."

"Not you. Your mum," said Staff. "You should do the class; your mum should take it easy."

"Oh yes, of course."

There were two more classes after boxing, the first one to take place on the beach. Mum insisted on coming down with us, but instead of leaping around on the beach, she sat down on a rock and watched as we did what Staff A called "sand training."

In case you were wondering, 'sand training' is when you do lots of activities that are hard enough on solid ground, but you do them on soft sand to make them so much harder.

Mum looked like such a sad, lonely figure, sitting there on the rocks, holding an ice pack to her face, but she insisted that she was OK and just wanted to watch us. The group members had all gone up to her one by one to commiserate and say how awful it was that she got hit in the face. With every comment of support she received, I felt like I was being indirectly castigated for my role in the whole thing.

"OK," said Staff A. "Welcome to "sand training". Can you all line up to face me, please."

Staff A stood with his back to the sea, allowing us to look over at the waves as they crashed down onto the beach while we worked out.

"Let's start with 20 jumping jacks, followed by 20-star jumps, run to Staff B and back, and repeat."

Oh, God. This weight loss camp was about doing the same tortuous exercises repeatedly in different environments. Giving the sessions different names like 'sand training', 'hill training' and 'park work out' just convinced the trainers that we were doing lots of different things.

I was the last one back, of course. They were all running on the spot while they waited for me. I was exhausted already. I looked over at mum longingly. I wish she'd punched me in the face instead.

Next, it was burpees and running with high knees - we did one minute on, the 30s off, for six minutes until I thought I might die of exhaustion. The knee lifts meant me whacking my knees into my enormous breasts that bounced around furiously inside my t-shirt even though I was wearing two bras.

After the aerobic exercise was over, I heaved a huge sigh of relief...until he said it was time for press-ups, planks, holding squats, and leg raises. I was soaking wet, thoroughly exhausted and - oddly - slightly exhilarated. Weird. I wouldn't say I liked it, but I loved how it made me feel.

MEETING TRACIE

*I*t was time for lunch. THANK GOD. After we'd eaten, we would be talking to a visiting lecturer. The thought of a lecture was quite appealing, and I never thought I'd think that. But anything that involved sitting down rather than doing star jumps and press-ups was fine. And the afternoon activity was a long walk, so at least that shouldn't involve any heart attack-inducing bursts of energy.

Lunch was carrot sticks (I KNOW!!!), with a few pepper and cucumber sticks and a small bowl of homemade hummus.

While we ate, a tall, slim, ferociously heavily-tanned and made-up woman came in. She must have been mid-50s but was dressed like a young teenage girl, in the brightest pink towelling shorts and a white t-shirt with white pom-pom socks inside wedge-heel trainers. Her hair was a bright, artificial blonde - almost white and down to her bottom and her lips were so inflated that they entered the room half an hour before the rest of her. And that's before we got onto the quite extraordinary breasts that looked like they belonged to a woman eight times her size.

It was as if she'd been beamed down from another planet. She looked like Barbie doll's heavily-tanned mum. We all sat there and stared, feeling wildly underdressed in our sweaty old tracksuits.

Staff A jumped up and went over to welcome her. I glanced at Yvonne, the most glamorous-looking woman in our midst, and followed her gaze as she took in the woman in front of us. Yvonne's face was an absolute picture. She didn't like this at all. I felt she didn't like Staff A being so attentive to the new arrival. I was starting to believe that Staff A and Yvonne were having an affair.

"OK, can I have your attention?" said Staff A. "I'd like to introduce you to Trace, who will do a series of short talks about health and fitness issues that you can take back into your everyday lives with you. Tracie, over to you...."

A small burst of applause led Tracie to bow deeply and unnecessarily. "Hiya, so I'm Tracie, and as you've been told, I'm here to give you a few talks over the next few days, mainly about nutrition and the value of thinking about what you eat and not following fad diets, but also about exercise and why it's so vital that you bring regular movement into your lives."

"This could be hysterical," said mum, adjusting the ice pack on her eye so she could see Tracie properly. "There's no way she's a nutritionist."

"I know," I replied. "This could be really good fun."

We sat back in our seats. Out of the corner of my eye, I could see Donald staring at Tracie like a man possessed. His mouth had dropped open, and a little drool had escaped from the side.

"The first thing I'd like to do is address some of the concerns I know you'll have. Who is this woman before me? What does she know about food? I know I don't look like a nutritionist...I don't look wholesome and well-educated and as if I spend my time growing herbs and making healthy meals. That's because I don't...but I know all about nutrition, and I have many ideas for making your diet and lifestyle healthier without too much effort.

"I was born in England, but my mother is French, and when I was 13, we moved to France...people in France have a very different approach to food, and I will be incorporating some of that thinking into my talks to you over the next few days."

She handed a pile of notes to Simon, and I glanced at Donald, who was still staring like some maniac. I felt a pang of anger at his obvious interest in her. I thought he was supposed to fancy me. He was trying to get me to stay in his room for one minute, but when a new woman arrived, he was all over her. Not that I was remotely interested, but - you know what it's like - it still smacks a bit when someone goes off you. I enjoyed being liked more than I realised, perhaps because it's so rare.

"Are you OK?" Tracie asked Donald.

"I'm fine," he said, jolting himself out of his reverie and turning to look at the note that Simon had handed to him. "Fine."

"OK, as you can see on the sheet, I believe strongly in movement. Not necessarily going to the gym or intensive cycling classes - just movement.

"I think one of the first things you need to do if you want to lose weight is to make your days as inefficient as possible. I know that sounds crazy, but you'll build exercise and move-ment into your day by doing things less efficiently. So - go the long way round to the bus stop and pace while waiting for the kettle to boil.

"Most people in Europe sit still too much. Research shows that those who move more, even if it's fidgeting or pacing around, are fitter and healthier than those who don't move.

"Let me tell you this - on average; obese people sit for two and a half hours more each day than lean people. In addition, lean people stand and walk for two hours a day more than obese people. How does that make you feel?"

She paused, waiting for someone to answer.

"I feel as if I ought to be fidgeting a bit more," I said. "You know - moving around."

"Yes. No one's saying you have to run a marathon every day or even continue to do the exercise classes you're doing here today, but try to move more. If you're sitting down to watch tv, get up in the adverts and do some tidying up or walk up and down the stairs a few times. Suppose you've got a pile of three things to take upstairs; take them one at a time. If you've got three bags of shopping in the boot - don't do that macho thing of trying to bring them all in at once - bring them in one at a time. Make your life more inefficient."

"This is better than I thought," mum whispered. "Make lots of notes for your blog."

"Oh yes, God - I forgot about the blog," I said, grabbing her pen off her and scribbling notes onto the side of the page. "Remind me every day. I must start putting posts up as soon as I get back."

"OK, just a few other things to think about," said Tracie; she used her hands a lot when she spoke, displaying finger-nails that were about 4" long. Some of them were pierced and had jewels hanging from them. "There are the obvious things that you all know about - park as far away from the place you are going to as possible and walk the final bit, get off the bus a stop earlier, use the stairs rather than the escala-tors...you know - everyday things that make a real difference.

"Also, why not set the timer on your phone to bleep at 10 to the hour, get up and walk around for 10 minutes, then sit back down and continue working? It'll make such a difference if you do that as often as you can throughout the day. Does that make sense?"

She seemed to look directly at me as she said it, so I nodded. It did make sense, to be honest. I knew I would never be a gym bunny or someone who became obsessed with attending exercise classes regularly, but I could easily jump around for 10 minutes every hour.

"OK," said Staff A. "We'll be hearing a lot more from Tracie over the next few days; we just wanted her to introduce herself and give you a range of things you can do at home to continue the good work you've done here. Now, if anyone wants to take a comfort break, go now, and we'll head off on our three-hour walk in 10 minutes. We'll be back in time for dinner."

LEARNING ABOUT WEIGHT LOSS

$\mathcal{M}$um and I wandered out of the villa onto the beautiful sun-dappled street outside, ready for our huge walk. It would have been so good to lie by the pool with a picnic, but - no - more movement was demanded of us.

"What did you think of her?" I asked mum.

"She was better than I expected. I suppose I learnt a few things."

"The main thing I learnt, mum, is that if you have too much filler and too much of a boob lift, you'll look like Barbie."

The two of us cackled, then heard a sound behind us.

"Hello, how did you find my talk?"

Mum and I jumped and spun around to see Tracie standing there. Hopefully, she hadn't heard us talking. From the smile on her face, it didn't look like it.

"It was great," said mum. "Really good."

"Yes, very useful," I agreed. "Just what we needed."

I noticed she'd changed into proper trainers and no longer wore the platform shoes she'd been in earlier.

"Christ, what happened to you?" she said to mum.

"Oh, that's nothing," said mum. "It's just where Mary hit me."

Tracie looked at me in disbelief, waiting for an explanation.

"I didn't hit her," I said for what felt like the 100th time that day. "I accidentally caught her on the side of her face in a boxing class earlier today. That's all."

"Oh, dear. I hope it gets better soon. You'll have a real shiner there," said Tracie, taking my arm and mum's arm and pulling us close. "I want to walk along with you girls."

We followed behind the crowd of bodies ahead of us, turning sharp left to go down the concrete steps onto the beach. It was a very stunning place... such an open, welcoming beach. As soon as you emerged from the stone stairs, there it was in front of you - the magnificent sea, painted the loveliest blue as if in a van Gogh painting, and miles of sand, fringed with cliffs at the far side. The sky was the colour of dreams - not a cloud in sight and no sound of anything but the gentle lapping of the water. And, to be fair, the whole place looked much more beautiful when you didn't have to do star jumps, and burpee jumps on the sand.

"Come on, you lazy buggers, speed up," said Staff A, completely ruining the whole atmosphere.

"Is this what you do full-time?" I asked Tracie. "Going round to these camps lecturing on exercise?"

"I run my own company," she said. "It's health and fitness based, with some personal coaching thrown in. I'm based locally and work with several sports teams and exercise companies."

"Personal coaching - that's exactly what I need," I said. "I just find it so hard not to eat stuff that's bad for me."

"It's not your fault, dear," said mum. "The amount of fat

and sugar they put into food these days is hard to avoid. It's not your fault."

"Oh, but it has to be," said Tracie, stepping over a small sandcastle. "You have to take responsibility; it's the only way."

"How can she take responsibility when manufacturers shove a load of rubbish into food," said mum defensively.

"Don't buy it," replied Tracie. "If a manufacturer sells a product containing fat and sugar, you buy it and get fat. Whose fault is it?"

We walked along without answering her.

"Ultimately, it's your fault," she said. "And if you try to remember that, life will be much easier for you."

"How?" asked mum.

"Because the manufacturers are trying to sell food to you to make a profit. That's their job. That's what they are there for. And they know that the better the food tastes, the more people will buy and the more profits they will make. It has to be your job to check whether eating these products is doing you any good. We can pressure manufacturers to be more honest with us, but at some stage, you've got to be honest with yourself and realise that what they want to achieve and what you want to achieve are polar opposite things. You have to stop eating it. How are we going to stop you from eating it?"

Mum nor I replied.

"Well, one obvious way is by arming you with all the information you need to make sensible decisions around food. Shall I bore you with some facts and figures, or would you rather I shut up so we can concentrate on walking?"

We were heading up a hill, and though I knew there would be magnificent sights when we got up there, it was tough walking, and I didn't want to think about it any more than I had to. "Facts and figures please," I said. These would be useful for my blog posts too.

"OK," she said. "Britain is the fattest country in Europe; it's a problem. But a recent Tory party conference was sponsored by Tate and Lyle. Now, think about that for a minute. If the money so entrances the government that it can't see the damage that sugar is doing, who's looking out for you? I'll tell you who - you. It has to be you who looks after you.

"One in three children under 15 is overweight or obese, and things are getting worse. Companies are targeting kids with sugar, salt and fat from a very young age. Only you can stop it. Only you can say 'no - I'm not going to eat that stuff; I'm going to be strong and healthy and eat natural foods that are good for me."

"Yeah," I said. I knew she was right, but I was so exhausted I could hardly think, let alone speak. Tracie seemed to be practically skipping up the hill, oblivious to how steep it was. She wasn't remotely out of breath.

"You know what I was saying earlier about doing bits of exercise throughout the day? Well - you have to do that. YOU. If you don't, you'll get fatter and fatter. Companies are making it as easy as possible for you to access their food.

"Food is being delivered to our doors. Domino's pizzas and all those lovely big Chinese takeaways - are being handed to us on our doorsteps. It's the complete and absolute opposite of how we were meant to consume food. Human beings were designed to go out and hunt for food. You didn't get food without physical exertion first; that was how the body was designed to work.

"Now, the most physical thing you have to do is open the door. It just isn't any good for us; you need to try and make yourself walk around, walk to the pizza place at the very least!

"Another interesting fact for you - research shows that

the more takeaways there are in an area, the more you will eat. It's the same with all addictions; the more readily available alcohol is, the more problems people have with drinking. It's a very straightforward thing, but you have to control it. No one else will.

"Avoid takeaways, don't go anywhere near them. Don't tell yourself that you'll have a healthy dish, keep away from them altogether.

"Think about your body in terms of what it was designed for. It doesn't want to be crammed with fatty food and no exercise. It doesn't thrive like that. It won't last a long time like that. Next time you see an old person, look at what size they are. They'll be thin. Very old people are always thin because fat people die younger. That's how simple it is. It's not at all healthy to be fat."

We'd reached the top of the hill where the others were all waiting for us, looking down on the beautiful scenery below. You could see for miles - out to sea where boats bobbed on the water and right across to the other side of the cliffs. I breathed in the warm air and thought about how there was every chance that I'd die before getting down again. I didn't want to be fat; it wasn't like I was deliberately eating to get fat; I just was fat. It was as much a part of me as my slightly wonky eyebrows or the small scar at the top of my thigh.

"Have you always struggled with your weight?" asked Tracie.

"No - I used to be thin and fit. I was a gymnast when I was a girl and trained all the time."

"Oh wow," said Tracie, clearly amazed that there was ever a time when I would dance around in a leotard. "How did you find gymnastics?"

"Quite cruel," I said. "It's a relentless pursuit of perfection. It's a tough sport."

"Yes, the performance sports are," said Tracie with a

knowing smile. She'd probably been a dancer or something in her day.

"Portugal's very beautiful, isn't it?" said mum. "I never realised just how lovely it was." She turned to Tracie: "Have you lived here long?"

"No, I was born in England and lived in France when I was a girl," she said. "I didn't come to Portugal until I was in my 20s... chasing a man. An Englishman."

"Ah, that's why you're English is so good," said mum. "I'm always very jealous of people who can speak more than one language."

"You should learn then," said Tracie. "Teach yourself Portuguese; it's very easy."

"I'm too old to learn new things," said mum, sitting down on the grass and urging us to join her. Bottles of water were being passed around, so we waited patiently for them to reach us.

"I find I get so tired very easily. Once I turned 65, every-thing became difficult."

"Are you sleeping OK," asked Tracie. She sat next to mum and arranged her glossy orange legs so that you could see her towelling shorts to where her knickers would have been if she'd been wearing any. I noticed with dismay that the orange-tan colour didn't stop at the top of her thigh but continued up.

"No, not really. I get over-tired, I think. However much I do during the day, I never sleep much. Even on this holiday, Mary's been going to bed before me.

"Sleep's important," said Tracie. "You can do many things to get a better night's sleep. The main thing to start with is a sleep diary so you know exactly how much sleep you're getting. Then try going to bed and waking up at roughly the same time each day; that way, your body will get used to it, it will fall into a rhythm, and you'll fall asleep faster and wake up easier.

"The other thing to do is swing open the curtains, let the light in first thing in the morning, and take a brisk walk whenever possible. Doing four 30- to 40-minute walks a week helps people with insomnia sleep longer."

"I don't think I can be bothered," said mum. "I'm OK, you know."

"Oh no, you must. One large study that followed participants over a 5- to 10-year period found that people who slept less than 7 hours a night were more likely to be obese."

I smiled at her. "Do you have a handy study to quote for every occasion, or do you sometimes make it up?" I said.

"I have read many studies and have been giving talks on this subject for 20-odd years. I promise you; I'm not making them up."

We were told to get to our feet and run a little on the spot to get our limbs moving again.

"Shall I give you one tip that will improve your life?" said Tracie.

Mum and I looked at one another. "That would be nice," said mum. "Would your advice be to never go to a boxing class with your daughter?"

Tracie smiled. "Maybe that would be a good idea, but my main piece of advice to you, and I suspect this will be more for Mary - make sure you have 60 whole minutes without electronic devices every day. That's no phone, computer, television - nothing. For an hour. If you do that, you will see your health improve, your mood improves and - eventually - your fitness improve."

"Right," I said. "I can't imagine that."

"No, but you should. You'd be amazed at how your mind calms, and your stress recedes. You'll have a whole hour free every day...you could read, have a bath, walk, meditate or do all of them."

"I'll try," I said, but in many ways, what she suggested would be harder than anything else we'd done. A whole hour? Even at work, I didn't go for more than 10 or 15 minutes without a cheeky text from one of my friends or a look on Facebook. I'd try, though; I couldn't imagine how successful I'd be.

WHY DO WE NEED TO WALK SO MUCH?

*A*fter the lecture from Tracie, I tried not to use my phone for the rest of the walk. I didn't play music or Snapchat as I went along; I just enjoyed looking at nature. Blimey, the time dragged. Not because of the nature - the place was beautiful, just because I'm used to walking and talking at the same time as texting and messing around playing games. It felt like the walk went on forever without my phone to distract me.

When we got back, half of us collapsed in the sitting room area of villa one, and the other half decided that enough wasn't quite enough and started swimming in the pool. No need to tell you which half I was in. I lay slumped in the armchair beside mum, who looked utterly exhausted. Her eye patch had slipped a little revealing a very red, very closed-up eye beneath it.

"That's the end of your formal exercise for today," said Staff B, standing up before us. "If you want to do more, go ahead." He indicated outside at this stage, where ten or more nutters were racing up and down the pool. "Tracie's offered to answer any health or fitness questions you may have, but other than that, you're free to go, and I'll see you for our penultimate dinner tonight."

Tracie stood up. "This is nothing formal, but if you have any questions, I'd be very happy to answer them," she said.

"Why the hell are we doing so much walking?" said a small guy with little round glasses. I'd seen him at some of the classes, and he struck me as being very fit. "There seems to be an extraordinary amount of it. I walk every day at home, but just for 40 minutes at a time."

"Good question," I said, nodding enthusiastically.

"OK," said Tracie. "Well - it's a good way to see the place. Obviously, we're in a lovely part of the world...many of you haven't been here before and won't come here again, so it's good to take time to look around and see things. But in terms of fitness, the answer is very simple - we walk so much because walking is exceptionally good for you."

"I bet she's got a study that proves it," I whispered to mum.

"Let me prove this to you," said Tracie, and mum and I did a secret high-five. "Let me prove to you that walking can save your lives."

"Save our lives?"

"Yep," she said. "Does anyone know why?"

"Because you get your heart rate going and your limbs moving?" I ventured.

"Star pupil. Well done," said Staff B, moving to stand next to Tracie. Staff B was quite pale, and when he stood next to her, it threw into stark relief just how orange she was.

I looked up to catch mum's eye, but she was looking through the patio windows, watching the seagulls dance elegantly through the sky over the pool, straining to watch them with her one good eye.

"Sorry to interrupt you, Tracie, but we forgot to give you

your snacks earlier, so I'll hand them out to you now while you're listening," said Staff B.

"Oh My God - that's the greatest news ever," I blurted out rather too loudly, encouraging titters of laughter from those assembled. It suddenly dawned on me that the group here were the rebels of the course, the kids on the back seat of the bus, the ones flicking bits of paper at the teacher. The well-behaved kids were outside doing extra homework.

It was quite a jolly moment.

Then I was handed half an apple. HALF AN APPLE! And my mood bombed.

"Since I'm a star pupil, can I have a whole apple?" I tried.

"Nope."

Blimey, these people didn't know the meaning of the word 'snack'. They should see me hoovering nachos while watching Netflix.

"OK, the importance of walking," continued Tracie. She had turned down her half of an apple. She said she didn't want to ruin her dinner. "I need to start by telling you a story about bus drivers and conductors."

This wasn't the most promising of starts to a story, but I decided to bear with it.

"In 1949, Jerry Morris, a professor of social medicine in London, conducted a study comparing heart disease rates between London bus drivers and conductors. "The drivers and conductors were from similar social backgrounds; however, there was a marked difference in the rates of illness between them.

"Morris's study showed that conductors were half as likely to die from a heart attack as drivers. He wanted to know why. In the end, he concluded that on every working day, while drivers were typically sedentary, conductors climbed and went down 500 to 750 steps.

"So, more than 50 years ago, doctors realised that regular exercise throughout the day was a lifesaver."

"Gosh. That's interesting," said Simon.

"Yes - it's very interesting because the difference between the drivers and the conductors and their life expectancies was so stark. Back then, there were just two people working on every bus - a driver who sat in his seat all day and drove and a conductor who scrambled around - up and down the stairs, making his way among passengers and collecting fares at every stop.

"Seeing the results and working out why was one of the first times doctors began to appreciate the link between early death and inactive, sedentary life. Being overweight or obese wasn't taken much into account back then, as most people were of normal weight. The drivers in the study weren't any more or less overweight than the conductors. Now, a half century later, the link between a sedentary life and early death has been reconfirmed in dozens of studies worldwide. "Exercise is important...not just for weight loss or toning or anything like that, but for living. If you want to live a long and healthy life, exercise must be a cornerstone. Walking is excellent exercise. That's why we do so much of it on the course."

She paused at this stage as if giving us all time to take in the magnitude of what she was saying. A silence fell over us. I'd try and walk more when I got back. I could easily get off the bus early or something...be more like the conductor than the driver.

"Any more questions?" she asked.

I had one. I always have questions: "You said when we talked before that manufacturers were putting loads of sugar in our foods, and we needed to make sure we didn't buy it. Why do they do that? Surely if they just made food healthier, many of the western world's problems would disappear?"

"Yes, but their priority isn't trying to solve the Western world's problems. You are talking about commercial companies trying to make money, and they sell more food if it's laced with sugar and fats. That didn't happen in the past because we have different tastes today.

"The reason for this? And one of the big problems of modern living? Freezers. Yep. More than 95% of people have freezers in the UK, and much of the food we put in the freezer must be highly processed for it to survive. Doing this removes flavour, so you must add more sugar, salt and fat to get the flavour back and make them taste nice again. In the past, people just ate fresh food and bought fresh every day because they didn't have freezers, so they had to. It was a real breakthrough when families bought freezers and could store food, but - ironically - we are much healthier without them. The healthiest way to live is to buy fresh food every day."

Again, she paused, and I looked at mum, who was trying to fix her eye patch. Simon leaned over as if to lend a hand, but I batted him away before he could help. "I've got this, thanks," I snarled as he retreated.

"Everything OK?" asked Tracie.

"Oh yes, completely fine," said mum. "I'm enjoying listening to you. Do carry on."

"OK - well, just one final point about processing food is that it makes it easier for the body to digest. Do you remember what I said earlier about making life as difficult for yourself as possible? Making yourself use energy whenever you can? The same applies here - normally, you have to use energy to break up the food you eat. The body has to break up the various components and work hard to digest them, and a certain percentage of the calorific contact of the food is used up doing this.

"But if all the work has been done for you in the processing, then all the calories in the product go straight into your body without you expending any of them in breaking it down, so food becomes more calorific as a result.

"You need to eat healthy, unprocessed food whenever you can."

"What? Never use the freezer?"

"I don't have one. I don't think they're a good idea," said Tracie. "But if you've got a large family and rely on them, the tip is to make sure you eat fresh, healthy, unprocessed food as much as possible and only use the freezer for emergencies.

There was a lot of mumbling at this...a lot of displeasure at the thought of being unable to pull burgers out of the freezer and shove them straight into the oven at tea time.

"Any more tips?" asked Donald.

"I think that's about it for now," she said. "There will be more time to talk tomorrow."

"OK, so there's nothing else you do to keep yourself looking fit and...if you don't mind me saying...amazing, that we should be doing?"

"Oh goodness, thank you," said Tracie, blushing a little through her radiant orange skin. "I do take a low dose aspirin daily. That's not a bad idea as you get older. It's controversial, I know, and I wouldn't advise taking drugs for the sake of it, but a blood-thinning medicine like aspirin helps to prevent heart attacks and strokes. My sister had a stroke a few years ago, and I was classified as high-risk, so I take one daily. Aspirin makes the blood less sticky and helps to prevent heart attacks and strokes. One with breakfast dramatically reduces the risks."

BUM FLASHING

*D*inner on the penultimate evening was slightly better (but we're coming from quite a low point). Instead of the usual bowl of indescribably bad soup, we had salmon with broccoli and even a yoghurty thing for dessert, which tasted quite sweet and delicious. It was served in a tiny bowl the size of an egg cup, of course, so when I'd eaten it, I ran my finger around the inside, trying to get every last morsel out. Then I tried to put my tongue into it to ensure nothing was left, but mum took it off me and told me to behave.

After dinner, there was the usual bee-line for the sofas and the commencement of the games. It was like living in the past, in the days before televisions. But none of that bothered me because I was entertaining myself by watching Yvonne, and, as always, she got to her feet and said that she was leaving for the spa down the road.

I looked at mum. I wasn't sure whether she'd want to come on this expedition with me, given how exhausted she looked and given that her eye was now completely closed up and a rather unattractive shade of grey. But I thought I'd try anyway.

"Come on, Yvonne's gone - let's sneak out and follow her. I'm dying to know where she goes," I said, nudging her.

"Wouldn't it be nicer to sit here and drink herbal tea with the others?" she replied.

"No," I replied honestly. "Why would you want to do that when you could launch yourself into the night on an extraordinary expedition."

"Really?" said mum. "An 'extraordinary expedition' to see whether Yvonne is meeting up with Staff A? Good job you don't work for the secret service; you'd be blown away by the things they have to do."

"Are you coming or not?" I said, not dignifying her comment with an answer.

"Okay," she said wearily. "But only so I'm there to keep an eye on you if anything goes wrong."

"Fair enough," I said. "I wish I had camouflage gear and a head torch."

"Oh God," said mum. "Let's go."

We left the villa, claiming tiredness and said we were heading off to get an early night but turned left at the top of the street, and took the road to the stone steps which led down onto the beach rather than back to our villa.

"How do we know where to go?" asked mum. "We can't go to every bar in town."

"I don't think there are many bars," I replied. I did a recce by talking to Abi, and she said there were three cafes and a hotel. The hotel is where the gym and spa are and where Yvonne claims she goes. Let's start there."

"OK," said mum. "But I can't go in like this. Can you put my patch back on my eye for me? I'll scare everyone."

I helped mum to apply the cotton pad and large plaster, and we continued on our way.

"I'm going to have a glass of wine tonight," I said. "Just a small one."

"Really? What, and undo all the good work? Why don't you have a glass of water like I'm going to."

"Because I want a glass of wine. Come on; I've been so good all the way through - I haven't had any sneaked-in snacks or anything…" (ssshhhhhh….no need to mention the three packets of crisps - mum doesn't need to know about those. Oh, didn't I mention that it was three packets, not one? Sorry about that. But we've had such tiny portions it was the only way to cope with it all).

"OK, but just have a small one," said mum. We walked along the beach towards the seafront cafes, and I scanned the area as we went - looking out for Yvonne and Staff A. I didn't even know whether Staff had followed her this time because he hadn't been in dinner tonight, but I suspected he had. I peered out, watching for every movement. I felt like a fugitive avoiding arrest.

"There it is," I said, pointing to a large hotel that looked as if it had lovely sea views. It was very plush. I imagined that it would probably have a very nice spa.

"What are you going to do?" asked mum.

"Well, why don't we see whether they are in the bar?"

"OK," said mum. "Of course, Yvonne could be in the spa, and Staff A could be in his room doing press-ups or something."

"Yes, I realise that," I said. "But we'll never know unless we go and check things out."

"We should look in the spa first," said mum. She'd worked out that any investigation I headed would attempt to start in the bar.

"Or the main bar," I tried. "We could have a quick drink while making a plan?"

"No - spa first. That's where she said she was going, so we

should check that out. Then, if she's not there, we'll know she lied and can try and find her."

"OK," I said, quite impressed that mum had thought this through so carefully.

First, we walked into the gym and pretended we were hotel guests taking a look around. There was no sign of either Yvonne or staff A in there. It was a nice place. Very plush, with lots of equipment, screens flashing on every machine and music sweeping through the place.

There weren't many people there, and those who were didn't seem to be doing a great deal; it was more the sort of gym you were seen in rather than one you worked out in.

"OK, she's not here," I said to mum, stating the bleeding was obvious. "Let's check out the spa area."

So, we walked out of the gym and into the spacious, pine changing room - it looked and smelled like a giant sauna. There were steam rooms, a jacuzzi, saunas and a 'splash pool' leading off the main changing room - each one was behind a door. There was a big pile of fluffy towels outside each of the doors.

"You'll have to get undressed; you can't walk into the steam room like that," said mum, flicking her hand to illustrate my inappropriate clothing.

"Damn," I muttered. This was all getting to be quite hard work.

I slipped off my leggings and t-shirt and went to wrap one of the lovely soft, fluffy towels around me. Of course, it was far too small and didn't come near to covering me. I grabbed another one and tried to arrange the two, so I wouldn't expose myself to everyone in the steam room. Then I went in. The place was full of steam - which, I guess, is what I was expecting, but I hadn't thought through the fact that I wouldn't be able to see anyone in there. I sat down and waited for my eyes to adjust. There was just one woman in there. Considerably older than Yvonne. On to the next room. The sauna was easier to see in - three women, no Yvonne. Then I walked into the room marked splash pool.

"I'll come with you," said mum. She followed me through the door leading to two small swimming pools. The glass roof had been opened, so it was like being outside. There were about 20 people there - some swimming, but most of them lounging on sun loungers and reading or talking. Clutching my towels tightly, I walked around, checking each face, in turn, to see whether Yvonne was there. No. No sign of her. So, I walked back to the door, reaching to push it open so we could go back into the changing room. But reaching out for the door involved letting go of my towel. Before I could stop it, the first towel fell to the ground, quickly followed by the second one, meaning that my large bottom was exposed to all the splash pool users in the lovely Portuguese spa.

WHEN MOUTH-TO-MOUTH GOES WRONG

I got changed as quickly as possible and tried to forget about the fact that everyone in the spa had seen my bum.

"They weren't looking. No one noticed," mum kept saying to reassure me. But I'd seen the looks of horror and heard the gasps as my towel hit the floor.

"I'll need a glass of wine now," I said as we walked into the hotel bar.

"I thought that might be the case," said mum.

I didn't loiter when we entered the bar. I walked straight up and ordered a large glass of wine for me, and sparkling water for mum, then took a massive swig out of it and almost reeled from the power of the taste. I've drunk only water and three cans of coke since arriving in the country. The taste of wine almost knocked me off my feet.

"Gosh, these small glasses are big, aren't they?" I said to mum, indicating the size of my large glass and faking disappointment. "I'm glad I didn't have a large one."

"Golly, yes," said mum. "There's no way you'll be able to drink all that."

Does she know nothing about me at all?

"Come on - let's wander and see whether we can find them. I know you won't relax until you've seen them," said mum, taking a delicate sip out of her glass

We walked around, cautiously looking for Staff A and Yvonne. In my head, the plan was for us to see them but for them not to see us. I hadn't quite worked out how we were going to do this. I realised it would probably involve throwing myself behind a pillar or a pot plant.

We walked around several times, looking into all the nooks and crannies. I even went into the ladies to check and stood for an unseemingly long time outside the gents.

Nope. They weren't there.

"We'll drink these, then go to the other little bars on the beachfront," I said. "If they're not in any of those, then they are not in town tonight."

Mum smiled and shook her head at me. I know she thought I was mad, but it was quite intriguing how they sneaked out. And I didn't believe that they'd never met before this holiday; the way he reacted to her at the airport was straight out of Love Story.

We took our glasses over to a table near the window. All the tables around us were full of people chatting in groups, enjoying food and drink. There were bowls of fries, oven-baked brie and piles of chicken wings on the table next to me. I was dying to reach over and help myself, but I managed to control myself.

I just watched them instead. Staring at the woman as she put a potato skin loaded with cheese and bacon into her mouth.

"Stop looking like that," said mum.

"I can't help it," I replied. "It's torture sitting here next to them."

The woman eating the potato skins was English, as was

everyone else in the group. They chatted about people they knew from home and what they were up to. And I relaxed as the familiar sounds of people discussing Love Island and Brexit washed over me. I was starting to enjoy my evening away from the camp.

Then, suddenly, the woman I'd been studying started having a coughing fit. She fell to the ground in a dramatic fashion, holding her throat. She looked in considerable pain, but no one at her table did anything; they just looked around at each other. The woman was choking as she writhed on the floor - reaching up to them as if to indicate that she needed help.

I'd done a first aid course a few years ago, so I fancied my chances of keeping her heart going until the ambulance came. I jumped out of my seat and ran over to her, turning her onto her side and opening her airway to check whether she was breathing. I tipped her neck back and prepared to give her mouth-to-mouth.

"Call an ambulance," I shouted to mum.

I felt amazing. Invincible. I was Wonder Woman. I'd be in every national newspaper and probably on that morning TV show with Piers Morgan. I'd definitely go to Downing Street and meet the Prime Minister.

I leaned in to give the woman mouth-to-mouth and save her from certain death when she suddenly pushed me away dramatically. She used quite a lot of force for a woman who'd been at death's door two minutes ago. Then she sat up and wagged her finger at me: "What are you doing? Get off me."

"I thought you were having a heart attack or something. I was trying to help," I said. I was alarmed and confused at the odd reaction that my kind act had provoked.

"We're playing a murder mystery game, and you're completely ruining it."

"Oh, sorry," I said. "I thought you were in trouble."

"No. We picked names out of a hat earlier, and I'm the victim. I have to die. It's part of the game."

"Oh, I see. I'm sorry," I repeated as a couple more people joined their table.

"Oh, my goodness," said one of them. "That's the flasher from the spa."

Everyone at the table was now staring at us. Mum looked completely baffled. I don't think she knew what was going on.

"Come on, we're going," I said. Mum stood up, and the two of us spun around and walked dramatically away from the table...just as Staff A and Yvonne walked through the door.

"Hit the floor!" I shouted to mum as if a gun-wielding terrorist had just entered the building. We both fell to our knees and crawled under the table of the group whose game I'd just wrecked.

Staff and Yvonne walked to the bar.

"Quick, let's go," I said. Shouting 'Bye' to the murder mystery people as the two of us speed crawled to the exit, darted out and ran down the road, not stopping until we reached the beach.

"So, they are having an affair," I said to mum.

"Unless they are just friends?" she suggested.

"But then why would they sneak out, and why would she lie about where she was going?"

Mum shrugged as we walked back over the sand towards the stone steps. "It's odd. You wouldn't have put those two together - they seem such different people."

"I know. I think that's what's so intriguing. I bet he flew her out here, especially to see her. I'm glad we came down to find out; that has intrigued me all week. And thanks for coming with me," I said. "It would have been horrible if I'd gone by myself."

"No problem, my little flasher," she said, laughing as she said it. "Honestly, you should have seen their faces when your towel dropped. They were a picture."

"I thought you said no one saw…."

"Ah, yes - I lied about that. They all saw," she said. And we both burst out laughing.

MY LEGS WERE ACHING by the time I got back to the villa. It had been an action-packed evening: flashing, ruining a party game, then crawling out of the pub on hands and knees.

"Why do the oddest things always happen to me?" I asked mum forlornly. "Other people go through days without punching their mother in the face or anything. I wish I could be like other people. Did they see my bottom in the sauna? That's so embarrassing."

Mum burst into laughter, and before long, I was laughing soon. "It was the ridiculous evening, wasn't it?" she said through spluttering laughter, giving me a hug and sitting on the bed next to me. "Honestly…"

Then she gasped and pointed outside. Her mouth was wide open. I followed her finger and there - in our pool again - was the synchronised swimmer. She danced merrily through the water while the two of us sat on my bed watching her.

"She's really good, isn't she?" I said.

"Yes," said mum. "She's wonderful. I thought you'd lost your mind talking about women dancing in the pool. But look at her - she's there, and she's really good. Let's go and watch her from the poolside."

Mum undid the back door, and we walked onto the patio.

The same music was playing as the last time I'd seen her - gently drifting through the night air as she danced around. She pushed herself out of the water effortlessly as we walked towards the pool. Still, as we got close, the same thing happened…she leapt onto the side with considerable agility. She ran away, tearing off her sparkly swimming hat to reveal a streak of blonde hair, grabbing her music player and disappearing into the trees.

"Oh, that's such a shame," said mum, looking disappointed. "I wanted to watch her."

"I know, mum. Me too. Oh, hang on. She's dropped something," I walked to the edge of the pool and there lay her swimming hat…it was old-fashioned with small flowers on it, and not sparkly at all. It must have been the reflections of the moonlight off the water catching it as she danced that made it look like it was covered in sequins.

I carried the hat back to where mum was waiting. Inside the cap, the initials NSF/TM were sewn.

"I need to take it back to her," I said to mum.

"Well, leave it here - she's bound to come back when she realises she left without it."

"No - I want to find her - I want to know about her."

"Oh God," said mum, seeing the excitement burning in my eyes. "We don't have time for more spying missions. When are you going to go off and find her? Tomorrow is the last day."

"I'll go in the morning," I said. "I'm not doing boxing and combat training for three hours, that's for sure. I'm lethal."

"You're not lethal," said mum.

"Really? Have you looked in the mirror recently?"

Mum shook her head and climbed into bed. I lay back on mine, still holding the cap, my mind spinning with thoughts and plans about how I might find the mystery swimmer.

As I lay there in the darkness, unbeknownst to me, the lady came back and, silently, while mum and I slept, she scoured the garden looking for her cap. She looked through the shrubs and moved the sunbeds and deck chairs around, but it was nowhere to be found. Disappointed, she left, off into the night from whence she came.

IN SEARCH OF THE PHANTOM
SYNCHRONISED SWIMMER

I woke up the next morning for our final full day in camp, still holding onto the swimming cap. It took me a few moments to remember what the odd item in my hand was. I had clutched it all night, leaving my palm sweaty underneath its rubbery skin. I felt a wave of excitement when I saw it and shot out of bed, still gripping onto it. Today was the day when I would find synchro woman.

I went to where my phone was plugged into the wall, near the dressing table on the other side of the room, and called up Google to investigate. It was only 5 am - earlier than I'd been up all week. It was no surprise that when there was the prospect of physical exercise, I had no desire to get out of bed, but when there was a mysterious synchronised swimmer to locate, I was out of bed faster than you could say 'nose clip'.

Mum slept soundly beside me while I put the initials embroidered into the cap into Google, hoping that the letters would mean something; that they would reveal where the swimmer had come from. NSF/TM: the letters had to be the name of a swimming club or something.

But...Nope. Nothing. Next, I googled synchronised swimming clubs in the area but couldn't find anything. This sleepy region of Portugal was not awash with sporting amenities, certainly not of the water dancing kind, but synchro woman must be based locally, surely. I couldn't believe the woman came miles to use my pool. That made no sense at all.

There was a sports centre with a swimming pool in the area, and it seemed to be a short bus ride away, so I figured that would probably be my first stop. There must be someone there who could tell me where synchronised swimming classes were held in the area. They might even be listed on the sports centre's website, but it was impossible to tell by looking at it because it was all in Portuguese, not English.

I figured out I could get the bus from outside the beach-front cafes. It was only a few stops.

As I studied the bus route, I heard a small movement behind me as mum woke up. "Goodness, what are you doing up so early?" she asked.

"Trying to work out how to find the synchronised swimmer," I said.

"Mind if I put the light on?".

"Of course not. I'm only sitting in the dark, so I didn't wake you."

Mum switched the light by her bed, and I looked over at her.

"Oh. My. F&$%ing God," I screamed. "Oh, Christ."

"What?" Mum looked perplexed.

"Your eye!" I said. "It looks like you've been in a fight with Mike Tyson...and lost."

Her eye was black and completely sealed up. It was puffy and tender looking. It did look like a boxer's eye the day after a fight.

"Oh, then it must look worse than it feels," said mum. "It's a lot less painful today than it was yesterday."

"I think you need to see a doctor," I said. "Do you want to come with me today on a hunt for Synchro Woman, and we'll find a doctor?"

"I'm sure there's no need," said mum. "And if this is your way of co-opting me into a chase around the country looking for someone whose face we've never seen and whose name we don't know, you can forget it."

"No, I'm being serious, mum," I said (and I was). "I'll forget the hunt for the synchronised swimmer - we'll go and get you to a doctor. We should have gone yesterday. Honestly, it looks really bad."

"But surely the people on the course would have suggested a doctor if they thought I needed one."

"Yeah, you'd think so," I said. "But they're all army people, you could probably lose a leg, and they'd get you to hop through the exercises. They don't do 'injuries'."

"I suppose so," she said. "But it doesn't feel too bad at all. I'm sure it'll be perfect in a couple of days."

"But what if it's not? What if it's infected, and you lose an eye and have to walk around wearing an eye patch for the rest of your life? Won't you wish you'd been to see a doctor then?"

"Yes, I suppose," she said. "And I can't do three hours of combat training this morning, can I? Let's go and find a doctor."

"Good, I'll see if google knows where the nearest one is," I said.

"And I suppose we might as well make some initial enquiries about the synchronised swimmer while we're out and about. I know how keen you are."

"Oh good," I said, rubbing my hands together in glee as I got ready. "I'm SO keen. You have no idea. That'll be fun. I know where the local sports centre is and how to get there;

we should start there in our hunt, but only when I've worked out whether the nearest doctor's surgery is."

We walked the now familiar path and headed down the stone steps and across the beach to find the bus that would take us to the local sports centre.

I had googled medical centres and discovered that next to the pool complex was a parade of shops in which there appeared to be both a doctor's surgery and a pharmacy. It struck us that if we went into the chemist's shop first and talked to the pharmacist, he or she could advise us whether we should see a doctor. The pharmacist might even be able to let us know the best way to get an appointment.

The bus journey was extremely short - just a couple of stops - it took about 10 minutes to get there, and both mum and I looked at one another knowingly. We should have walked it. "What have they been saying to us all week?" said mum. "Walk whenever you can."

"Yes, I agree," I said. "We'll walk back."

My excitement about finding the synchro woman had now mounted to such a fever pitch that I would have promised to walk to the moon and back. I was ready to go inside and begin the search. I had the hat tucked into my handbag and mum by my side, looking like a pirate in her large, black eyepatch. What could go wrong?

We queued up and waited patiently at the main reception, with all the children clutching their towels as they bought tickets for a morning swim.

"I wish I spoke Portuguese," I said to mum. "Even just a few words would make it easier. I don't know how I'm going to explain to this woman what I'm after."

"I was thinking the same thing myself," said Mum. "If she only speaks a few words of English, "synchronised" is unlikely to be one of them."

Once we reached the front of the line, the excitement

turned to panic as I realised I had to explain my desires to this woman, and there was no doubt that I was going to sound very odd.

"Synchronised swimming," I said, waving the hat around. "Is there anyone I can talk to about synchronised swimming?" I said.

The woman looked at me blankly.

"Synchronised swimming," I repeated as if that would help. Then, the inevitable happened.

"Show me," she said.

"OK," I replied and began leaping around in the reception in my best interpretation of a synchronised swimmer. I had a fixed smile, sudden upward jumps and even a few high kicks to convey my message. The entire row of children and most of the people in the café opposite were watching, intrigued by my sudden performance.

Remarkably, the woman in reception seems to understand me.

"Ah," she said. She looked again at the hat, and a look of genuine comprehension passed over her face.

"I understand now. Down to the end on the left. Is there."

"Who is there?" I asked.

"Person of the hat."

"The person who owns this hat is here?" I said. I couldn't believe it. I hoped they'd be able to translate the letters on the hat for me or advise me where to go next; I never expected to be directed straight to Synchro Woman's office.

"Come on," I said to mum. "We're in business."

"Wonderful!" said Mum. "And astonishing that she knew what you wanted from that little routine in reception."

"Cheeky," I said. "That was a magnificent display of floor synchronised swimming, even if I say so myself."

We walked towards the room that we had been directed

to by the lady at reception when we passed a ladies' toilet, and mum said she had to go.

"Really? Can you not wait?"

"I'll be two minutes," she insisted.

I waited patiently for way more time than was necessary for someone to go to the loo. I had no idea what on earth she was doing in there. I just wanted to go and find the synchronised swimmer. So, I walked down to the room the lady had suggested we go to and knocked gently on the door. There was no answer.

"Hello, is anyone there," I said.

I turned the handle cautiously, and the door opened into a small room that looked like it had been set up for fitness testing. There were scales, callipers and measuring tapes. I slammed the door shut quickly. I didn't need to see callipers and weighing scales. Urgh. It was like a torture chamber in there.

"There you are!" said mum, who had emerged from the ladies' toilet and was wandering down the corridor with a familiar-looking woman.

"Look who I found in the ladies," said mum, indicating Tracie standing beside her.

"Hi, how are you doing?" I said. "Have you heard about our mission?"

"Indeed I have," said Tracie. "And I'm going to accompany you. I know exactly where you need to go; follow me...."

And so, the three of us walked confidently through the sports centre, me waddling along, Tracie striding confidently ahead, orange skin gleaming in the sunshine, and mum shuffling along pirate-style beside us.

"In here," said Tracie, indicating a door that was nowhere near the one that the receptionist had told us to go to. She knocked gently on it, but there was no answer; then she knocked again.

I'll peek in," she said, turning the handle, but the door wouldn't open.

"Damn, it's locked."

We all stood there looking at the locked door for a little while until she had a brainwave.

"I know," she said. She marched off again with the two of us running behind her and spoke to a small, tubby woman in Portuguese.

"Follow," said the woman, leading the way through the sports centre. She had an oddly wide gait for someone so small, and as she walked, she had her hands resting on her hips. She looked like a cowboy who'd just got off his horse.

"She knows where to go," said Tracie. So, we followed John Wayne through the centre, still searching for the owner of a rather fancy synchronised swimming cap.

The woman led us to an office right back at the back of the building.

"Thank you so much," I said as she opened the door and talked to a tall man inside. They had quite a conversation before he said.

"I take you."

So now there were five of us on our mission, walking around the building. The very tall man, the small, fat woman who walked like a cowboy, mum looking like a pirate, me waddling along to keep up, and Tracie with her bright orange, Day-Glo legs.

He took us to another room, but that was empty too. Where on earth was this woman? An unfeasibly tall man spoke to Day-Glo legs woman while the cowboy lady watched and nodded. Pirate and I just looked on forlornly. There was a lot of shrugging and raised voices.

"No one knows," Tracie said eventually.

"OK," I said, a little confused. "The receptionist said it was that room at the end of the corridor, right where you come into the centre."

"Oh," said Tracie. "Right - let's go back there then."

So, back we all trouped, through the sports centre, dropping off the man and woman who had accompanied us (but been no use at all) as we went. Then we followed the corridor back, and I said: "There, that's the room the lady in reception said was the right one."

"No - that's not right. That's my room."

"Your room? So, you work here?"

"Yes - I do the fitness and nutrition for the squads here."

"Oh. How odd."

"Look, don't worry. We'll find a first aid person somewhere," said Tracie. "They are probably just busy treating someone."

"No - we're not after a medic," I said.

"Yes - for your mother's eye," said Tracie. "I thought that's what you had come for - to find a medical specialist."

"Oh, no, that's my fault," said mum. "I must have confused you when you asked about my eye, and I said we were going to find a doctor. We're actually at the sports centre on a more complicated mission."

"We are here to ask about synchronised swimming. I found this cap," I said, pulling the swimming hat from my bag.

Tracie practically swooned in front of us and leaned heavily against the wall. "Where did you find that?" she said, her eyes wide with excitement.

"It was left by our pool," I said.

"That was your pool?"

"Yes, a lady has been doing synchronised swimming in the pool outside our villa. She left this hat, and I wanted to return it to her."

"That's me," said Tracie. "That's my hat."

"It's YOU," both mum and I declared. "Why did you run away when you saw us?"

"I didn't know it was you. I thought you were coming to tell me to get out of your pool, so I got out before you could tell me off."

"We were coming to watch you...you were brilliant."

"Oh," said Tracie, all smiles. "Thank you. That's so sweet."

"How did you learn to do that?"

"It's a long story," said Tracie. "Shall we get some herbal tea?"

"That would be great," I said. "But first, let's go to the pharmacy to get mum sorted; then, I want to hear all about this."

LEARNING THE TRUTH ABOUT
NSF/TM

*T*he three of us went to the pharmacy around the corner from the sports centre, where a very friendly pharmacist said he thought mum's eye was best left alone. He recommended painkillers and some antibacterial eye drops to keep it all as clean as possible and told her to visit her GP back in England if it hadn't improved over the next couple of days. He also recommended regular ice packs and getting lots of rest. Mum nodded gratefully and bought the drugs he advised.

Then it was time to hear Tracie's story.

"I was a very talented synchronised swimmer when I was younger," she said as we sat sipping some revolting green tea in the cafe near the sports centre. "I competed for France; then in 1987, I was selected for the World Cup, held in Egypt."

"Oh, my goodness," said mum. "That's amazing. You must be really good."

"I was very good," said Tracie. "But I struggled with terrible stage fright and was never very good in the big tournaments. I just froze. That's what I did in the World Cup...I panicked, and I fell out of synchro. We were on for a medal and could have won gold, but I messed up, dropped out of the medals, and came fourth.

"That's the worst place to come...to miss out on a medal. It was awful. And it was all my fault."

"Oh no," said mum, "I'm sure it wasn't all your fault. It can't have been."

"Yep," said Tracie, nodding vigorously. "All my fault. I did a completely different routine than the others - I forgot everything."

"You shouldn't beat yourself up," I said, though I did make a mental note to try and find a video of that World Cup - Tracie doing a completely different routine to the rest of them sounded hysterical. "Fourth in the World Cup is brilliant. The World Cup is probably like the Olympics of synchronised swimming. That's brilliant."

"Yes," mum said. "Really brilliant. Well done."

"Well, it's strange you should mention the Olympics because they took place the next year," Tracie said, looking even more mournful. "And I was selected. I couldn't believe it. I had another chance."

"Oh, that's fantastic," I said. "I love a story with a happy ending."

"Yeah, except I was so nervous when I got there. It was in Seoul, and I'd never been anywhere like that before. I was just terrified...and I did the same thing again...I messed up, and France missed out on the medals. We came fourth. Again."

"Oh dear, I'm so sorry," said mum. "Though - you shouldn't blame yourself. It's natural to be nervous performing in front of all those people."

"You're very kind, but it was awful. I stopped the sport as soon as I returned to France and never did any synchro again until about two weeks ago. The guys at the sports centre

117

found out about my background and were keen for me to start running synchronised swimmer classes. I froze when they first asked me and said there's no way I could do it, but Rodrigo - the guy in charge here - told me to think about it...and the more I thought about it, the more I thought that I'd quite like to do that. But I didn't know whether I could remember anything, so when I came to the camp to give the talks and saw all those empty pools, I thought I'd come back at night and practice while you were all having dinner. I didn't want to ask anyone in case it drew attention to me. I just wanted some time in the pool to check whether I was still comfortable in the water."

"You certainly looked it," said mum. "You were impressive when we saw you."

"Thank you," said Tracie. "I loved it. I loved every minute of it, and I'm going to teach lessons at the swimming pool and try and build up a young squad."

"That's amazing," said mum. "I'm so pleased. And I'm sorry if we scared you off when you were practising - we didn't mean any harm at all - we just wanted to watch because you were so good."

"Thank you," said Tracie. "That's kind of you."

I handed the swimming cap over. "Sounds like you're going to need this," I said. "Just one more question - what do the letters inscribed on the inside mean?"

"Oh - they are from my international days - so synchronised swimming in French is nage synchronisée, and the 'f' is for France because that's who I was competing for. My name is Tracie Molton, so: NSF/TM is the national team and the swimmer."

"Got it," I said.

. . .

DESPITE MUM and I saying that we would walk back, we got a cab with Tracie in the end. She was coming over to join us all for our last evening in camp. We sat comfortably on the back seat and watched the beautiful scenery rush past us.

"That thing in the sports centre was quite funny when you think about it," I said. "You and two senior members of staff in there all joining in the hunt for you."

Tracie smiled. "Yes, that is very funny. I was just asking everyone where the first aid person was."

"I'll miss this place," I said.

"Will you miss all the exercise?" mum asked.

"Nope."

I looked over at Tracie, who seemed lost in her own world, presumably reliving that moment at the 1988 Olympics when it all went wrong.

"Do you have to do a lot of exercise to lose weight?" I asked. "Only I do hate it?"

"Yes," said mum. "Which is best - exercising or dieting to shed the pounds?"

"Well," she said. "You'll be relieved to hear there's been a study."

"Hooray!" said mum and I.

She laughed. "I'm not that bad, am I? Forever quoting studies."

"No, not bad - it's good," I said quickly. I'm delighted that you've read all these studies."

"Good, well - this was a big study - done in the UK, featuring more than 300,000 patients. They asked: 'Can weight and inactivity be considered separate risks?' In other words, you can still exercise and still be fat, and you can be thin and not exercise. One does not depend on the other.

"So, the study showed that regular exercise will reduce many health risks associated with being overweight and inactive, but might not directly lead to you losing weight. You have to change your diet to do that.

"This ties in with the other studies that have been done - remember the bus conductor and bus driver study?"

"How could we forget?" I said.

"Well, that was done because drivers died earlier, not because they were fatter than conductors. Exercise is important for health and longevity. And you know what else is important?"

"Ooh, do tell," I said.

"The regularity of that exercise. So, if you sit and look at the computer screen for eight hours solid without moving, then go to the gym for an hour, that's not as effective as doing an hour, then some exercise, or having regular exercise breaks through the day. The human body was designed to move."

"So, it would have been ideal if the bus conductors and the drives swapped jobs every hour?" mum said. She can be so wise sometimes.

"Yes - absolutely - that would have saved lives."

"Could it have been stress as well?" I offer. "I mean - I get that exercise is healthy, and it's important to build movement into your everyday life, but if I drove a bus every day, I'm sure it would be the stress that killed me."

"Back during the bus driver study, stress was not appreciated as a health risk, but you're right. Things like tight schedules, traffic jams, angry passengers, filthy air and other factors would have been a factor. A life packed with unrelenting stress is far more dangerous than a few extra pounds."

I nodded, smiled, and thanked her for her input, but inside I was thinking, 'if I give up work and have no stress in my life, I can eat chocolate all the time.'

WHEN MRS A TURNED UP
UNEXPECTEDLY

*I*t was dinner time. Our last dinner of the trip. It had all gone by so quickly. I'd hated it in many ways, but in others, I'd loved it. I'd learned so much and was looking forward to putting it together in the blog posts next week in the hope that it could help other people.

We walked up to the dining room tables and looked around, working out where to sit. "Hey, come and sit by me," Yvonne called out, tapping the seat next to her and causing me to feel all sorts of anxieties. Did she see mum and me crawling through the hotel bar last night, trying to escape without being seen?

"Come on," I said, dragging mum away from where she had stopped to talk to Simon. I noticed he had his hand on her arm as he spoke to her.

For God's sake, will that man never stop?

"Come on, mum, come and sit here."

I treated Simon to an angry scowl and indicated to mum where we would be sitting. I took in the shock as she looked at Yvonne and back at me.

"Had a good day?" she said to Yvonne in a rather forced manner.

"Yes, a lovely day, thank you. And you?"

"Yes, it's been great," said Mum.

"How's your eye feeling now?"

"Much better, thank you. It looks much worse than it feels."

"I didn't see you both this morning," she said. "Did you decide to take it easy?"

"I went with mum to find a doctor," I said. "Then we ended up going on a bit of a mission."

Despite promising myself that I would keep my synchronised swimming story to myself, I couldn't help it.

"Oooo…do tell," said Yvonne. I paused my revelations while the chef delivered an unbelievably bland-looking bowl of what I assumed to be soup, but looked like slosh, then continued once he'd left.

"Well, there's been this great mystery in our villa," I said. "When I returned after the first night, do you remember I went back early because I haven't been very well?"

"Yes, I remember," said Yvonne. "You fell with an almighty thud, and we all thought you died."

"I prefer to think of it as me having delicately fainted, but yes – I collapsed. And when I went back to our villa…."

"I need to stop you there," said mum. Will these people ever stop interrupting my story? "You went back to the wrong villa and climbed into Donald's bed."

"Yes, after that, when I got back to my villa."

"Hang on, so – the rumours about you and Donald are true? I assumed they weren't…."

"What rumours? No. No. Nothing is going on between Donald and me. I went back to the wrong villa, went into what I thought was my room and got into bed. That's all."

"And Donald got in beside you?"

"No. I woke up when he came in and left."

"That's not strictly true, is it?" said mum. "You did stay there for a bit and chat with him when he was in bed."

"No, look – this is all a distraction. Do you want me to tell you my story about what we got up to this morning? It's far more interesting than any half-made-up tale about me accidentally going back to the wrong villa."

"Okay, sorry – carry on," said Yvonne. "We can come back to your love affair with Donald later." She nudged mum, and they giggled at this point, but I was determined not to be thrown.

"Well, when I got back to my room on the first night, the room felt really stuffy, so I opened the patio windows."

Are you sure you weren't just all hot and bothered from your night of passion with Donald?" said Mum.

"No, I was hot because my roommate had forgotten to put the air-conditioning on."

"Oh yes," said Mum. "I just thought it was such a waste of money to leave the air-conditioning on when we were there. It hadn't occurred to me that it would be like a sauna when we returned."

I glared at mum, but Yvonne put her arm around her conspiratorially and said, "It's an easy mistake to make. Almost easy as accidentally getting into a man's bed."

"Can I carry on with my story now?"

"Yes, go on, dear," said Mum.

"When I stepped outside and wandered towards the pool, I could see a woman doing synchronised swimming."

"What?" said Yvonne. "That's so weird… How could there have been someone in there doing synchronised swimming?"

"I know! It was very odd. I sat on the edge of the sun lounger for a while, just watching, but when I moved closer to the pool, the woman saw me and swam like a mad thing towards the edge, climbed out and ran away into the trees. I stood up and went after her, but she'd disappeared."

"I thought she'd gone completely mad," said mum. "You know these people who collapse, have a bang on the head and are never quite the same afterwards? We thought that's what had happened to Mary."

"I knew I was right, though," I said. "I watched for five or 10 minutes, and she was really good; I knew I hadn't imagined it."

"Okay, so what happened next?" said Yvonne. I'd piqued her interest.

"The same thing happened the next night, and again I was on my own, and when I told mum, she thought I must have lost my mind. But then last night, mum was with me, and we saw the swimmer again in the pool."

"Oh, and she was wonderful," said mum. "Very beautiful; gliding through the water in the moonlight, she looked like someone in the Olympics, you know, with a sudden spring up out of the water with a mad smile? She was doing all of that."

I explained to Yvonne how we walked over to stand near the pool to get a better look, and the swimmer saw us and fled again, but this time she left behind her swimming cap and inside were these initials…'"

Just as I was about to continue with the story, Yvonne's phone buzzed into action, and she looked down at it, where there was a text message.

"I'm so sorry, I'm dying to hear the end of your story, but I have to go. Can you tell me all about it at breakfast?"

"Sure," I said, glancing at mum, who immediately looked at me. "I'll tell you the end of the story in the morning."

"Okay, I'll see you then. Sorry to run out. Have a lovely evening."

With that, she was gone, speeding out of the villa.

I looked at mum. "Well, I think we know where she's going," I said. "She must have gone to meet him again. You can't tell me that she suddenly, desperately felt the urge to have a sauna."

"No, you're right, dear," said Mum.

"And, by the way - stop mentioning the whole Donald thing. Nothing happened. It was a simple mistake."

"OK," said mum. "And synchronised swimming woman didn't even come that night, did she? It was the night afterwards."

"Well - good. Then even less reason for you to mention it."

As we sat there looking at one another, we saw Staff A leave. He walked calmly out of the room and then ran up the stone steps, turning a sharp left at the top.

"Do you think we should follow them again?" I said to mum. "It worked out so well last time."

"Ha, ha," she said. "Which bit of it did you think worked out well then?"

"You know the one thing that confuses me about their affair - why aren't they sneaking back to his room? Why would they run off and then just sit in a bar? It seems crazy."

"Yes, that is odd," said mum. "Unless they have a room in the hotel?"

"Oh yes. That's probably what they're up to. Oh, go on. Let's follow them again. It's such fun," I said. "I get a real thrill from it. Today was hysterical - finding Tracie. I can't believe how that happened."

As mum and I sat there chatting, a middle-aged woman appeared in the doorway with an overnight bag, looking around, confused. She wasn't anyone I recognised from the course, and she didn't look like she worked at the villa.

"Hello, are you looking for Abi?" I said.

As I spoke, Abi came out of the kitchen and saw the lady.

"Anne!" she cried. "How lovely to see you; I didn't realise you were coming."

The two women hugged warmly, and she put down her bag.

"I wasn't planning to, but I thought I'd surprise him. I thought we could spend the evening together."

"Oh, he will be delighted," said Abi. "I'm not sure where he is. Let me see if I can find out."

Abi disappeared, and Anne sat herself down at a table near the door.

"How are you feeling then, now we're at the end of the week. We managed to get through it all with only a few minor disasters," said mum.

"OK. I quite enjoyed it in the end, except for boxing. Dad's going to have a fit when he sees your eye," I said.

"I know. I have warned him what to expect when he picks us up at the airport."

As we talked, Abi came up to us. "Have you seen Staff A?" she asked.

I looked at mum, and we both looked back at her.

"I think he might have gone for a walk," I said.

Neither of us wanted to lie, but neither wanted to say where he was in case he wasn't supposed to be there.

Anne stood up from the table and walked over to join us.

"This is Anne, Staff A's wife," she said.

"Ohhhh!" I said.

"Nice to meet you," mum said in a much more controlled fashion.

Then Simon walked over. "I think he's gone down to the hotel bar by the seafront," he said. "He pops down there most evenings to catch up with friends."

"Okay, let me get my jacket, and I'll take you down there," Abi said to Anne. "I'll just be a minute."

Abi went to get her jacket, and I looked at mum.

"Shall we go," I said to her while grabbing my hoodie, nodding at Anne, and speed walking towards the door?

"Where are we going?" said mum, running to catch up with me.

"We have to warn them," I said. "We can't let his wife walk in on them."

"OK, you go ahead. My laces are undone. I'll do them up and be right behind you."

I ran ahead of mum, which was as much a surprise to me as to her. Somehow, I was given speed and strength by the mission to get to the romantic lovers before Anne. I ran like the wind - across the gravelly paths and over the grass verges, then down towards the seafront bar on a mission to save a man's marriage.

THE TRUTH ABOUT YVONNE

I burst into the bar, where Staff A and Yvonne sat, holding hands over the table and looking at one another adoringly.

"Hey," I screamed as I fell towards their table, barely able to talk after all that running. "Move apart, move apart," I shouted. "She'll be here any minute."

Everyone in the bar looked up as I confronted them. I was red in the face and sweating profusely as I started physically manhandling Staff A to move him away from Yvonne.

"Mary, what on earth's the matter?" I couldn't move him. I was panting like a wild animal on a hunt.

"Your wife. She's here," I said, motioning between Staff and Yvonne. I noticed they hadn't stopped holding hands, so I leapt in and yanked their hands apart. "For the love of God - do I have to do everything?" I asked as I saw mum and Mrs A coming into the bar.

"Your wife," I said dramatically, sweeping my hand back to indicate her arrival before I whispered to Yvonne. "You better run. Quick. It's his wife."

"Hi Anne," said Yvonne, getting up and hugging the woman. "Have you met Mary?" she said.

"Very briefly," said Anne, nodding in my direction.

"Is everything OK?" said a man from the table next to us. When he recognised me, I looked up to tell him everything was fine. "It's you," he said. "The woman from last night - the one who flashed her bottom at everyone in the sauna and crawled out of the bar on her hands and knees. I'm amazed you have the cheek to show your face again."

"What?" said Staff A.

"Oh, it's nothing, nothing at all. Mistaken identity," I said.

The man saw mum standing there and gasped. "My goodness - what happened to your eye?" he asked.

"Oh, that? That's nothing," said mum. "Mary punched me in the face, but it's much better now."

"Punched you in the face? What sort of animal are you?" he asked me.

"Look, it's fine," said Staff A, standing up and putting his hand out to show the man he wanted him to back off. "I can deal with this."

"You need to run, Quickly," I whispered to Yvonne. "Go now. Save yourself."

The man returned to his table, and Staff A pulled over several chairs.

"Take a seat," he said. "Let me get you a drink."

"Oooo. A drink? What - a proper drink?"

"Yes, I'll get you a proper drink. What do you want?"

I ordered a large glass of wine and sat back in anticipation. Mum said she'd have a cup of tea. Yvonne got up and walked to the bar with Staff A while mum, Mrs A and I sat there in horrible, painful silence.

. . .

"OK, so what's this all about? Why have you come charging down here and attempted to pull me out of my seat? And what's all this about you flashing everyone in the sauna?" asked Staff A, handing me my drink.

I decide not to address the sauna incident. "To be honest, I thought you and Yvonne were having an affair, and when your wife arrived in camp, I thought I ought to come down before her to warn you. Although, I'm guessing that's not what's going on here, is it?"

Staff A exploded into rip-roaring laughter and put his arm around me in a friendly fashion. "Oh Mary, you are funny. Yvonne's half my age, and I've been happily married for 30 years. This woman has stuck with me through thick and thin; I'm not about to mess her around now."

He and Anne held hands and looked at one another.

"But you've been secretly meeting every night, and you said you didn't know Yvonne when you picked her up at the airport, so I knew you weren't friends...I suppose I just assumed...."

"I didn't say that I didn't know her - I said that I'd never met her before. Look, even though I've never met her, I feel like I knew her so well because her dad always talked about her."

He trailed off at this point and looked at Yvonne. "Do you mind if I tell them," he said.

"No, that's fine," said Yvonne. "I don't mind at all."

"OK, I've been in jail for the past six months. I was locked up after an incident in Afghanistan. I was accused of mistreatment of prisoners...something I never did.

It was a horrible time. I was accused of things no one wants to be accused of."

"Waterboarding?" I asked, remembering Staff B's reaction when I had used the word in jest. "Was it something to do with that?"

"I'm not going into any details, Mary. If you read that in the press, I would ignore anything else you read because I was cleared of everything."

"No - I didn't read anything in the press," I said. "Honestly."

"OK, well, the facts are that I was found guilty and locked up, but then evidence emerged which proved that I didn't do it, indeed couldn't have done it. That's all I'm saying. I was freed three weeks ago and didn't return to the army.

"While I was in prison, there was a guy there who saved my life. He kept me strong and urged me to keep up the appeal. He was Yvonne's dad. I said that I would meet up with her when I came out and check she was OK. Then I got this job, which seemed like the perfect one for me. But I wanted to see Yvonne, so I thought the best thing would be to get Yvonne to come out here. We've been meeting so I can tell her all about her dad in prison."

"Oh," I said. "Gosh, I'm sorry. I didn't know - I was trying to help, you know. I didn't want Anne to walk in on you. I just...sorry...."

"It's fine," said Yvonne. "I would have told you about it if you'd asked."

"Oh," I said, turning to mum. "I never thought about asking. Did you?

Mum shook her head and finished her tea.

"Shall we go back," I said. "Leave these good people to talk."

"Yes," said mum. "I think that's probably for the best. We've done enough interfering for one day. We must pack; we have an early flight in the morning."

"OK, see you both before you leave," said Staff A.

"You won't be up that early, will you?" said mum. "We have to leave at 7.30 am to get our flight."

"Yes - I'll be up. I'm weighing you first thing, remember. We'll see how much weight you've lost."

"Oh yes - how exciting," said mum. "I'm dying to find out."

"Yeah," I said, regretting the sneaky coke, crisps and jelly babies and Mars bars (OK - I didn't mention the Mars bars and jelly babies, but I knew you'd judge me harshly if I did).

FINAL RESULTS

$\mathcal{I}$ stood before the scales like an Olympian about to step up to the start line in the Olympic 100m final. The only difference was that this athlete knew she'd been cheating...sneakily eating and drinking through the week when people weren't watching: coke, crisps, Mars bars and jelly babies. I know - it's terrible, and I'd only cheated myself, but I couldn't have survived on the rations they gave us. Honestly, I'd be dead now. Dead. And the staffs would be up for murder. Would they want that in their consciences? No, they wouldn't. Their lives would be ruined by it. I was doing them a favour by eating, saving them from misery and guilt.

I knew I had eaten far less than I usually would and exercised a tonne more but still - I couldn't have lost more than a few pounds.

I'd sat there as others in the group had lost up to 6 lbs. I knew I'd be looking at 2 lbs at the most. I was hit by a sudden rush of disappointment in myself and anger that I hadn't done this properly...just for four days to see how much weight I could lose. But then there was the whole 'I might die thing. Maybe this was better.

"On you pop then," said Staff A, like this was some fun adventure I was engaging in.

I stepped onto the scales and watched the numbers whizz up...12 stone, 13 stone, 14 stone...then it slowed down. It stopped before 15 stone. "You're 14 stone 7lbs," said Staff. I looked at him as if he'd taken leave of his senses.

"That's insane," I said.

"It's pretty good going, Mary. You've lost 9 lbs. You're our biggest loser. Well done! Your mum lost 5lbs, and you've lost 9; that's a whole stone between you."

There was a ripple of applause behind me and a small shriek of excitement from mum, and they presented me with a floral headdress bearing the words 'biggest loser'.

"Thank you," I said. "This has been the most glorious and interesting trip ever."

I turned to Staff A, gave him a big hug, and said something I never thought I'd say: "Thank you for pushing me and believing in me."

"Any time," he said.

Mum and I hugged everyone before leaving, and Staff B came out to our cab carrying our bags.

"You're a superstar," I said, hugging him tightly. "Thanks for your support."

"It's been a pleasure," I said. "We're all looking forward to reading your blog."

"Ha, ha," I said. "Then you'll know exactly what I got up to."

"Indeed," said Staff B, closing the door for us and giving a mock salute as the car drove off.

"When does your blog go up?" asked mum.

"In two days," I said. "When I'm safely out of the country."

"What are you going to write in it?"

"I'm going to write about everything," I said. "Every last

detail, but mainly I'm going to say how brilliant it was and how much I learned. It was brilliant, wasn't it?"

"It was fantastic," said mum, giving me a gentle hug. "Thank you for taking me."

"You were right about the carrots, though. I don't think I'll ever eat one again…."

HOMEWARD-BOUND

*W*e got onto the plane back to England, refreshed and excited after our trip. I felt closer to mum than I had for years, which was an unexpected advantage of her coming with me. I also felt lighter and happier than when we boarded the plane a week ago. It was wonderful what a break like that could do for you. I felt so much more positive and confident. I'd pushed myself, and it had paid off.

Unfortunately, my happy mood dissipated when we arrived at Heathrow, expecting to see Ted there to pick us up. Every time I have collected him from the airport after one of his trips, I've arrived there early and held out a banner to welcome him. I hoped he might do the same for us, but there was no sign of him.

'Where did he say he'd meet us?' asked mum.

'Right by where we come out. That's where he usually is.'

'Perhaps he's waiting somewhere else. Send him a text; love. See where he is.'

I pulled out my phone and saw a message from him. He'd sent it while we were on the plane.

Can't get there to pick you up. Have to stay at work. Perhaps your dad could collect you? Will have to work this weekend, but let's try and catch up next week.

My stomach lurched as I read it. I knew he was busy at work, and we'd not been great recently, but this was a real shot to the head.

'He's not coming,' I said to mum. 'He's busy at work.'

'Oh well, don't worry.'

'This is a rubbish thing to do,' I said. 'He knew what time the plane was. He knew we'd already be on it. We could have rung dad if he'd let us know this morning. I'm getting fed up, mum.'

And that's when I burst into tears. The disappointment of being let down by him felt all the more acute after our special week away. I'd looked forward to seeing him and telling him all about it.

'Don't worry, angel. We'll get a taxi.' she said.

'It's the end of our relationship. I can't do it anymore. I'm really fed up.'

'Come back to ours tonight; we'll talk about it, love. Then we'll have carrot soup.'

'Not funny, mum. Not funny at all.'

TWO MONTHS LATER

OOPS THERE GO MY KNICKERS

*O*h, hello. I'm afraid you've caught me at a rather indelicate time; I'm lying on my back, knickers discarded somewhere in the room, while a handsome man touches me in the most private places. Yes, you read that right. Me, half naked with a man. He leans closer to me, and I wriggle a little, adjusting my hips on the bed.

"Everything OK?" he asks, promising to be as gentle as possible.

"Yes", I say, with a moan in my voice as he hits a particularly delicate part. "Yes, I'm OK."

He looks up and smiles warmly at me, then flicks off his sterile gloves.

"Right, all finished," he says. "That wasn't too bad, was it? Slip your clothes back on, and I'll see you in a minute."

God, I hate having smear tests. I mean, I know they're important and lifesaving, and anyone who's had cervical cancer will warn strongly that not having them and getting cancer is a hell of a lot more painful and terrifying than a quick 20 minutes on the doctor's couch every two years...but - bloody hell – I hate them.

I pick my clothes up off the chair, searching for my knickers. Where are they? I look back on the chair, but there's no sign of them; I turn my trousers inside out, but...no. Christ. Where have they gone? I put the rest of my clothes on, without the knickers, and check one more time before walking through the curtains, to see the doctor sitting at his desk.

"Before you go, let's just do your blood pressure," he says, inviting me to sit down. He pushes up the sleeve of my left arm and wraps a band around it. He inflates the band until it is tight and peers down at the numbers on the dial. Then he looks at me quizzically. "It's quite high," he says. "Did you know you had high blood pressure?"

"No," I say, and I know what's coming next.

"It might be an idea to get your weight down and do a bit more exercise."

"Yes," I reply.

"I know that's boring, but every little pound lost and every 10 minutes of exercise you can do will make a big difference in the end."

"OK. I will try," I say, but it's going to be hard over the next few weeks; I've got Juan Pablo coming to stay. Remember him? He was one of the dancers I met on a cruise a while ago. We formed the most unlikely friendship after bonding over a 90-year-old called Frank. We ended up stranded in Europe when we missed the cruise back - it was a real fiasco. Anyway, we stayed friends, he came over briefly at Christmas, and now he's coming over to visit for the month, and I CAN'T WAIT.

"Are you under any kind of stress?" continues the doctor. "Anything that's worrying you that could have caused your blood pressure to rise?"

I look at him blankly. Ted and I finished our relationship a few months ago, and I'm devastated. I can't sleep properly, I can't think straight, and I'm self-medicating with Domino's pizzas.

"No, I say. "Everything's just fine."

"You don't look sure," says the kindly doctor, peering over his glasses in a very doctorly way.

"I've had a tough time, but I've got a good friend coming to stay and will get out of my rut in no time."

"That's good to hear," he says. "I suggest you return in a couple of weeks just to check that your blood pressure is stabilising."

"OK," I say, standing up. "Thanks, doctor. Oh - one thing I should mention - I can't find my knickers anywhere...they must be somewhere in the cubicle."

"Oh, right, fine, of course," he says. "I shall look out for them."

TED AND ME

I walk out onto the street and phone Charlie
straight away.

"It was a bloke," I screech at her.

"What?"

"A bloke. Doing my smear test. Why on earth do they
have men doing them? It was so bloody awful."

"It might be the only action you'll get for a while the way
you're going, so you better enjoy it."

"Oh, thanks very much," I say. "You're supposed to be my
best friend."

"Well, if you won't date anyone, the smear test will
become a special time in your life. Was he nice?"

"Not nice like that, no. Nice for a doctor. I can't even
remember what he looked like, to be honest. He was kind of
bland. And I wasn't exactly looking into his eyes."

"No, fair enough. That would be weird," says Charlie.

"I don't like it when male doctors do smear tests, though.
I find it uncomfortable."

"Me too," said Charlie. "You should have specified that
you wanted a woman."

"Yes, but then I feel like I'm a huge pain."

"Na. It would be best if you told them. Tell them next time. As I said, you might appreciate the attention if you're still single next time you have a smear. You might be asking for a male doctor."

"Will you stop it," I say? Honestly, she's been moaning at me constantly since Ted and I split up after the weight loss camp with mum, insisting that I should 'Get Back Out There' and meet someone new before I start seizing up completely. "But I still love Ted," I told her numerous times.

"Well, then go out with him."

"But it wasn't working with him."

"Well, go out with someone else then."

"I don't want to; I love Ted."

"I will come over there and bash you across the head in a minute. You're being very annoying."

The truth is that I still love Ted, but I don't know whether I want to be with him. Well, when I say that, what I mean is - I want to be with the Ted I first met...Ted was attentive, funny, and a joy to be around back then. But then our relationship started to feel stale, and as if it was continuing out of habit rather than love, things got more and more difficult.

Ted works really hard, which I love about him, but it means we hardly ever saw each other, and when we did, he was on his phone half the time. He was always exhausted and didn't want to do anything, and I just got bored by it. I think he did, too...we seemed to get on each other's nerves all the time.

Then, there was the night when it all came to a head. We had spent the evening at his flat bickering and getting annoyed with each other. I was cross that he hadn't picked mum and me up at the airport after our health retreat, and he was cross with me for not understanding how busy he was. It was dismal, and I felt sad, frustrated and angry all at the same time. I remember looking at him and thinking, for the first time in our relationship - I don't want to be here. I looked at my watch and wondered how I could get out of there without it becoming a huge drama.

"You want to go home, don't you?" Ted said.

I looked at him. I didn't want a massive confrontation; I just wanted to leave.

"Be honest with me, "he said. "Let's just stop pretending this is working and be truthful with each other."

I burst into tears at that point, of course, because it was a hideous situation that I didn't want to have to deal with. I loved him. I still love him. There was, and is no question about that, but I find it frustrating when I am in his company because he doesn't seem to love or cherish me like he used to.

"I do want to go home," I replied. Eventually, tears streamed down my face. "But I love you and want to be with you; I don't want us to split up or anything."

"We don't need to split up," Ted had said. "But I've got quite a lot on now; I need to focus on work. Perhaps a little break would give us both time to think. Let's meet in a couple of weeks when I've got through this conference and all the meetings, and we can see how we feel then, okay?"

"OK," I said reluctantly. "But promise me you won't meet someone else and forget about me forever."

I know, I know. It was deeply pathetic.

"I won't meet anyone else, you idiot. I love you," he replied. "But perhaps we've been spending too much time together and just got bored or something. I don't know, but I know that we are sitting here bickering and you keep looking at your watch and clearly want to be at home, so you should go."

"It's not that I want to be at home," I said, which wasn't strictly true. What was strictly true was that I didn't want him to want me to be at home, and I felt all troubled and upset now he'd suggested it. Is everyone like this, or is it just me?

"Come on; I'll drive you," he insisted.

It felt like all the power in the room had shifted. Now he wanted me to go home, and I didn't want to. I'd rather sit there feeling miserable, as long as it was in his company than be at home by myself, feeling alone and unwanted. Tears were pricking at the back of my eyes. I reached for my cardigan and stood up reluctantly, following him to his car like a sulky teenager.

"We're going to be okay, Mary," he said. "Remember that, okay? We're going to be together forever."

"Forever," I'd replied while choking back tears and trying to stop feeling anxious and scared.

After that, things just seemed to get worse. I returned to my flat and called Charlie because a situation like that calls for a chat with your best friend. She came around and stayed with me while we drank wine, ate pizza, and I sobbed. "There's nothing to get upset about," she kept saying. "You're still with him; he's just taking some time to finish his work projects, then you'll be back together again - like you should be: Ted'n'Mary.

"Yes," I stuttered, unconvinced while crying and blowing my nose.

The next two weeks crawled past, and finally, the day arrived. Ted and I were going to meet up and be back on track.

Charlie sent me a cheeky note saying 'I bet he proposes' and my mum phoned to wish me well. It felt like there was quite a lot riding on this date which, with hindsight, wasn't very helpful. I felt pressured to get the relationship going again as soon as possible.

I dressed up, of course, and set out to meet him, looking as nice as I could.

We met in the pub, and when I walked in, he was on the phone and barely acknowledged me. My heart sank. I'd spent an hour and a half curling my hair and £50 on a new dress. He couldn't even say 'hello'.

He seemed so distracted and horrible. I mean – not horrible – because Ted's never horrible, but it felt like he would rather be anywhere else on earth. When I said this to him, he looked angry.

"What do you want me to do?"

"I don't know, be a bit enthusiastic," I said.

He shrugged and told me he was doing his best, and it was ridiculous that I now wanted to control his mood. He said he'd had a difficult day at work; I just had to take or leave him. At that moment, I felt like screaming, "leave you then", because I was just so disappointed that he wasn't as excited about seeing me as I was him. I'd been looking forward to this moment every day for the past fortnight, and now he was ruining it.

We sat there in silence after that, Ted sipping his pint and me getting crosser and angrier and more and more upset.

Then he looked at his watch. "Come on, let's go," he said.

He dropped me home, gave me a peck on the cheek, and said he had to get back and have an early night because he had to go to work the next day.

I felt like I'd been shot. I'm sure my heart dropped a little. I know this is pathetic, and it doesn't necessarily mean you are being rejected when a guy says he's got a lot of work on. But it hurt. Ted never had too much work on to stay the night when we first met; now he did. I just felt as if, on this one occasion, given we hadn't seen each other for two weeks and were fighting to keep the relationship going, he could have pulled out all the stops and made me feel special, making me feel we should be together again.

I pictured him turning up with a big bouquet of flowers, whisking me off somewhere wonderful and having a picnic he'd prepared. Instead, he'd asked me to meet him in the local pub, spent half the time on the phone, and then dropped me off without wanting to come in. Come on - I know I can be a drama queen sometimes, but that's not right. That's not how someone behaves when they're in love with you.

He'd made me feel as if he was only there because he had to be and not because he was desperate to see me.

After the paltry kiss on the cheek, he left, and I went and lay on my bed. Later I sent him a text saying I realised he was very busy at work and that maybe we should leave it for now and aim to meet in a few weeks. Then I ignored his texts for a while, didn't take his calls, and by the time we spoke a month later, I said I didn't feel the same about him. That was about a month ago. Now we're in limbo; we've sort of split, but nothing's been clarified. I remember one time, near the beginning of our relationship, when we had a row, he turned up at my flat and sprinkled rose petals everywhere. Not this time; he's just stayed away.

My friends have been quite disappointed in him, which is why they're urging me to get out there and meet someone new. But - I don't know. I kind of want to be with Ted.

THE ARRIVAL OF JUAN

*I*t's 6 pm, and Charlie and I are at Heathrow airport awaiting the arrival of the lovely Juan Pedro. I can't believe he's coming to stay again; it's been a while since I last saw him, though we have been Skype-ing regularly, and we've kept up with each other's news.

I've been trying to explain to everyone what Juan is like...how he's very flamboyant and peacock-like but also warm, tender and very kind. I've explained that he's great fun and a bit crazy, but also the sort of person you can rely on. Charlie met him at Christmas, of course. And she'd heard a lot about him before that. When I returned from my three-week cruise, I couldn't stop talking about him and showed her all the incredible pictures of him, dancing on the stage in his sparkly trousers and out on the town at night in his sparkly trousers.

"He looks just as glamorous off stage as he does on," said Charlie.

"Yep...just you wait til he comes for the month," I replied.

The truth is that Juan is an absolute nutter. He is the loveliest, kindest man – flashy, loud and gorgeous. In short, he is exactly what a girl needs when she's been suffering from heartbreak. I'm dying to introduce him to everyone.

It flashed up on the board that his flight landed a while ago, so now we're just waiting for the sight of my glamorous Spanish friend amidst the sea of returning holidaymakers in their ill-fitting shorts and raspberry ripple legs. Then - he's there – as magnificent as ever. He's got white blond streaks through his dark hair, which immediately makes me think of a badger, but besides that, he's exactly the same. He wears mirrored sunglasses and wiggles in trousers, a few sizes too small for him. It means that every step he takes is tiny, so he's doing lots of them to keep up with everyone, dragging his bag on wheels behind him, and causing all eyes to swivel in his direction, just as he likes it.

He's wearing tight black and red striped trousers which finish just above his ankle, with red loafers, a red belt, and a skin-tight white T-shirt. In his left hand, he clutches a bright red, felt Fedora, and in his right hand is his immaculate, bright red case. He must be the only man whose suitcase matches his hat. You've got to give the man credit; he does nothing by halves on the sartorial front.

"Hello, my gorgeous angel," he says, thrusting his bag at Charlie and wrapping his arms around me. He seems so genuinely pleased to see me that it cheers me up.

"I have been sooo looking forward to this day," he says. "You look magnificent as ever. How have you been, my little chickadee?"

I don't answer his question because I don't want to ruin the moment with talk of my collapsed relationship. Instead, I turn to Charlie and reintroduce him. She smiles warmly at him as she takes in the splendid sight before her.

Juan hands me his hand luggage before looking Charlie up and down. He looks at her from the front, the sides and the back and tells her she is still as beautiful as she was when he met her at Christmas and that if he weren't gay, he would marry her straight away. She looks delighted and tells him that were he not gay; she would be thrilled to accept his proposal.

"We are the three amigos," he says, striding off across the concourse. Charlie is pulling his case, and I am holding his hand luggage as we sprint after him. Meanwhile, Juan throws his bright red hat onto the side of his head and steps ahead of us. If only he had a cane, he'd be like Willie Wonka leading us through the chocolate factory.

It's only about a half-hour drive from Heathrow to my flat, but Juan manages to embarrass us about 50 times during it, leaning out of the window and doffing his hat at everyone we pass. He is shouting at people and telling them that he likes their coats, hair or car. We finally pull into my road, and I'm giddy with relief.

"Well, that was pleasant," he says. "I met lots of new people. Now, remind me... which apartment is yours?"

"It's this one," I say, pointing to the rather rickety white gate leading down to my neighbour's flat and a couple of steps up to mine. "Mine's the top flat."

"Flat," says Juan to himself. "Top flat. We're definitely in England now, aren't we?"

It's left to Charlie and me to unload his bags from the car and take them inside while Juan surveys the street and seems quietly to approve of it.

"Nicer than I remember," he says, hugging me affection-ately. "I knew you'd live somewhere lovely, but I hadn't remembered it being so very English and so very quaint."

"Ahhh," I say, hugging him back. I'm inordinately fond of my little flat, and I'm glad he likes it too.

Once inside, I head for the kitchen and pull a bottle of wine out of the fridge, pouring generous amounts into each of the glasses. I can hear Charlie and Juan chatting away in the sitting room, and it gives me great joy that they enjoy each other's company. It's always great, that isn't it...when you know people from different areas of your life, then when they meet, they get on.

I walk out with the drinks, and Juan demands that he sees the bottle before he lifts the glass to his lips.

"You haven't got a clue what one wine is like over another," I say.

"No, but I have to keep up the pretence," he says, mimicking a British accent. Having feigned a check of the label, he takes a huge gulp of his wine and sits back.

"How's the love life then? Back with Ted yet?" he asks.

"Nope. It's over," I say. "I haven't seen him for months, and he's not remotely interested in me."

"But are you interested in him?" Juan asks.

"No," I lie, avoiding Charlie's eye.

"Is there someone new in your life?"

"No. There's no way anyone would be interested in me. Look at me," I say.

"What?? You're beautiful. Any man would be proud and honoured to be with you."

"Well, no one has made any approaches to me. I will be old and grey and living here surrounded by cats in 20 years."

"You will be if you continue sulking like this," says Charlie. She turns to Juan: "I can't get her to come out; she should be meeting new men and having fun, not hanging about at home, hoping that he returns to her."

"I've not been hanging around at home," I say. "I've been chilling."

"I think we need to get her back into the world of men, Juan," says Charlie. "We need Mary to get herself out there, internet dating, meeting new people and having fun."

"Well, of course. Por supuesto," says Juan. Let's get her online immediatamente."

By the time the second bottle has been consumed, a plan has been hatched: it's a plan that Charlie and Juan have cooked up for their amusement, although they are trying to convince me that this is all for me...to give me a bright and interesting couple of weeks.

"So, just to confirm," slurs Charlie. "Juan and I will put together a profile of you, then put it onto dating websites and come up with dates for you over the next two weeks."

"Right," I say. "Do I get to see the profile you put together?"

There's a small whispered discussion, and the verdict comes back: yes, I can see my profile, but the choice of men is entirely theirs, and I will only be given a small picture and a few details about each one before meeting them for a date.

"What's your lucky number?" Juan asks.

"I don't know - three."

"Oh, that's no good. Any other numbers?"

"Why do you want to know?"

"I do. OK, look - we'll multiply three by three to get nine."

"Right," I say. I don't know what's happening now.

"Nine will be your lucky number. We will organise nine dates for you over the next two weeks. All you have to do is turn up there. OK?"

"Oh God, OK," I say, mainly because it might be fun, and it would be nice to go on some dates, but also because I've drunk way too much wine and saying 'yes' is easier than fighting my way to a 'no'.

"I'm going to bed," I say, staggering to my feet. "See you in the morning."

"Yep," says Juan, pouring the remainder of the wine into

his glass and Charlie's glass. "We've got a bit of talking to do, but we'll see you tomorrow."

I give them a big hug and tell Juan how pleased I am that he's here; then I shuffle into my room and collapse on the bed. Oh lord. What on earth have I just agreed to?

PLANNING

I am up first the next morning and head into the kitchen to get a coffee. Juan is fast asleep on the sofa rather than in the spare room. I peer into the room he should be in - my tiny box room - and there's Charlie, fast asleep on the bed. How chivalrous of him. I don't know what time they were up until last night, but they both look exhausted.

I go over to the computer and hit the return key. In all its glory, there in front of me is the profile they created last night. There's a rather rough-looking photograph, but they have written nice things about me. I'm pleased to say that they have put the profile together as themselves, saying they are great friends of mine and think I'm the loveliest person ever. They say I'm kind and funny and want to be loved. That makes me feel all teary. I suppose I do want to be loved. I guess everyone does. Certainly, everyone embarking on internet dating. Why would you put yourself through all this if you weren't hoping to find love at the end of it?

The profile continues by saying that I'm a family person, a loyal friend and a one-man woman. That stops me in my tracks because it makes me think straight away of Ted: lovely, kind and smiley Ted.

Lower down; there are descriptions of the sort of man they think I'd like to meet: big, strong, kind and loving. All true, but - again - it feels like they are describing Ted.

"Oy, what are you doing?" says Charlie, appearing in the room in my nightshirt, which is about four times too big for her, making her look all little girl lost and pretty even though she's still wearing yesterday's makeup and her hair is all crazy and matted.

"Nothing," I say, jumping back from the screen as if she's caught me selling babies on the dark web. "Nothing at all."

"Dios Mio," shrieks Juan, arising from his slumber to find me at the computer. "You must not see the men."

"Calm down - I just looked at the profile, which you said I could look at anyway. I didn't look at any men. The profile's nice, by the way."

"Thanks," said Charlie. "Though we were blind drunk when we did it, we should check it makes sense."

"Shall I make some breakfast?" says Juan, sitting up sharply before lying back down again and holding his head.

"I'll do it," says Charlie, seeing him in distress.

"Have you moved in or something?" I say to her.

"Well, it's fun here," she replies. "I'll go if you want me to."

"I'm only joking," I say. "You can stay as long as you like."

"Good, cos I like plotting with Juan. I want us to find you someone lovely. Someone who makes you smile."

"Hmph," I reply. "Anyway, I thought we could go out for breakfast. I have to pop into the centre to collect some tax forms. PD11 or something. I can't do my tax return without it. Thought we could pop in and collect that and have breakfast at the centre...there's a nice cafe, and I get 50% off."

"Sure," say Charlie and Juan. But no one moves. Charlie sits on the end of the sofa and has her legs under Juan's duvet. There's no sign of us going anywhere for a while, so I join them too, and the three of us sit there, all warm and cosy, in my little flat with a big duvet over us, just enjoying life. Enjoying each other and the power of friendship. We could have stayed there all day were it not for my stomach rumbling loudly, followed by Charlie's, then Juan declaring that he didn't eat anything all day yesterday - he just drank a gallon of wine.

"Come on then, to the garden centre," I say. And we all rush off to get changed before piling into Charlie's mini. Now, I'm very proud of my friends, and I'm delighted to introduce them to my workmates. But when Juan emerges in a blue silk shirt, open to the waist and skin-tight trousers with bright blue peacock feathers all over them, with white, sparkly loafers, I wonder what on earth my colleagues will say. Juan is an incredibly exotic creature...it's like he's been beamed down from another planet. The people at work are – how do you say this? – very much of this planet. They are not very exotic at all.

In the end, of course, he is the biggest hit imaginable with everyone and has them all in stitches as he tells them about how we met on the cruise.

"And now I am going to help her find the man of her dreams," he says.

"Ohhhhh…" they all reply. "How are you going to do that?"

"Internet dating," he says proudly.

"Oh, you have to be careful of that," says George, the young lad who works in houseplants but is desperate to move over to hardware, so can usually be found amongst the hammers and screwdrivers, leaving the spider plants entirely to their fate.

"Why?" I ask. "My mate went on some online dates, and this time he met a girl, and they went out and had a lovely time until the end of the meal; there was food left over, so the waiter asked whether they would like to take it with them. My mate says: 'No thank you,' because - like - they are on a date. But she says 'yes' straight away, turns to my mate and says: 'My boyfriend can have that. I won't have to cook for him tonight.'

"No!" We all squeal in harmony.

"Yes," replies George confidently. "And it wasn't the only thing...The next day he woke up and went to his car, and the windscreen was smashed, and two of his tyres were flat. There was a message saying, "don't mess with my girlfriend". He'd never do internet dating again after that."

"Not as bad as what happened to my mate's dad," says Trevor, coming out of the storeroom and joining us for a chat. He stinks of cigarettes, and I feel like telling him that if he gets caught smoking in the storeroom, Keith will sack him. But I am more eager to hear his Internet dating story than I am to save his career, so I let him get on with his tale.

My mate's mum died of cancer, and a few years afterwards, his dad decided he wanted to meet someone new, so he went onto the Internet and made a date with this lady. He was so nervous before the date he almost cancelled it, but my mate assured him that it was a good way for older people to meet new partners, so he went ahead.

"They met for a drink at a pub and got on really well. My mate's dad thought she was a cracking bird, so he asked her if she fancied going for dinner. He pulled out all the stops and took her to that nice hotel on the river. Well, anyway, they went in there, and he pulled out her seat for her and every-thing - being all gentlemanly he was. She sat down, and he went and sat opposite her, and then she had a coughing and choking fit. She couldn't stop coughing. He kept asking if she was OK, but then she suddenly fell face down onto her plate.

"He wasn't sure whether she was doing some comedy

turn to start with, but then he realised she wasn't moving. He wasn't quite sure what to do. He went around the table to see whether she was alright, and a waiter came over to help, but when they tried to lift her face, it was no good. Anyway, to cut a long story short – she was dead."

"Dead? What the hell sort of story is that? What do you mean she was dead?"

"Brown bread. I swear on my life it's true, he couldn't believe it... The woman was dead on the spot. They called an ambulance and everything, and he went with her to the hospital, but she was dead before the ambulance arrived. It's a shame because he got on well with her sons when they turned up. He said they were a nice family. I think he went to the funeral and everything and fitted in well with them, so it's a shame she died."

SHOPPING

"Well, that was sobering," I say to Charlie and Juan as we sit in the café with our large breakfasts in front of us. "What if someone dies on me?"

"Not going to happen," says Juan. "We will select only young, fit, healthy specimens...not people who will die."

"If they are young and fit, they won't fancy me: look at me," I say.

Juan looks at me and shrugs. "You are gorgeous...any man can see that. I'm not sure about the outfit you're wearing. It looks like you are in your pyjamas, but besides that - you are lovely."

"I always wear t-shirts and leggings when I'm not out in the evening," I respond. "They are comfy."

"I know you always wear t-shirts and leggings. I looked through your wardrobe earlier...God help me - where do you keep your real clothes."

"I like dressing like this. These clothes are comfy."

"Yes, they may be comfy, but are they alluring...will they catch the man of your dreams?"

"No, I guess not," I say. "But if the man of my dreams

doesn't like me like this, the relationship will never work because this is how I dress. He has to like me for me."

"I understand that," says Juan. "But you have to make an effort. The man who comes to meet you might like to hang around at home naked, with his hairy balls hanging out; it doesn't mean he should come on a date like that, does it?"

"Christ, no," I reply.

"Well then...you need to make an effort just as he needs to."

"I guess…" I say, tailing off because I know he's right, but the thought of a man turning up for a date with his balls hanging out has made me feel a little queasy. I take a large sip of tea.

Juan calls up various outfits on his phone that he thinks I will like while I run my thickly buttered toast through the bean juice on my plate. God, I love breakfasts. I'm filling my mouth with the joyful combination of beans, butter and toast when my phone rings, and Dave's delicious face pops up on the screen. Dave is my neighbour; he lives in the flat below me and is staggeringly good-looking...like a young Elvis Presley meets a young Jose Mourinho. God, he's lovely. I went through a phase of being quite obsessed with him, going down to his flat every now and again, and letting him do naughty things to me, even though he had a girlfriend and would throw me out as soon as she called. But now we've settled into quite a nice friendship, and I enjoy his company. He was a decent guy beneath the chiselled jaw, with green eyes and ridiculously long eyelashes.

"What the hell was going on last night," he says. "Was there a party that you didn't invite me to?"

"No, just a couple of friends were over - you know Charlie and my friend Juan from Spain."

"Ooh, is she pretty? I like Spanish girls. Tell her to come down with her castanets tonight."

"Juan is a man," I say, and there's a moment of silence while Dave recalibrates after the thought of a night with a lovely Spanish girl disappears.

"What are you doing?" he asks. "Are you at work today?"

"No, I'm having breakfast with the guys, then I think we're going shopping in Kingston."

"We are going shopping in Kingston," shouts Juan.

"Can I join you during my lunch hour?" says Dave. I don't think he has any desire to come shopping with me, but he's curious about my group of friends.

"You don't want to come shopping with us," I say. "Honestly, we're just going to get a few outfits because I'm going to start internet dating."

There's silence at the end of the phone.

"Dave? Are you still there?"

"Internet dating?"

"Yep, Charlie and Juan are finding men for me, and I'm going to go on a series of dates. They think it's important that I get back out there after Ted."

Charlie and Juan are nodding at me as I speak.

"So, it's completely over with Ted?" asks Dave. "I thought you two were bound to get back together."

"Well, yeah, for now, it is," I say. "I don't know - I guess relationships are tough, aren't they?"

"Hell yes," says Dave. "I avoid them like the plague. Internet dating is no pushover, though...you meet some right characters on there. Make sure you don't let anyone get too close until you know them."

"Right," I say. I don't know what else to reply to. I mean - how could I let them get close before knowing them?

"People pretend to be something they're not. There's a lot of catfishing on there."

"Catfishing?"

"Yes. Or certainly kitten-fishing."

"Oh my God, Dave. What the hell are you talking about? I've never heard of any of these things."

"Do you want me to come up tonight and tell you about it?" asks Dave.

"Yes, please," I say. "Come up when you get back from work, and you can meet Juan."

"OK, see you around 6 pm," he says. "Happy shopping."

Charlie has to leave for work, so Juan has me all to himself for our shopping trip. He moves us from the table to the wicker chairs by the window and sits back, wrapping his legs around one other in a most unnatural fashion. He's double-folded them, so his legs look like they're plaited together.

"Is that comfortable?" I ask him. "You know - with your legs all tied in knots."

"Perfectly," he says, unravelling them elegantly. "Now - stop changing the subject and stop trying to distract me. We need to get some sexy outfits to throw into that wardrobe along with the oversized sweatshirts, baggy trousers and loose-fitting dresses."

"I did have some nice clothes. When I first met Ted, I dressed up all the time, but then I just got lazy, and it's hard when you're fat, Juan. You'll see when we go to the shops. There's hardly anything to buy, and my first thought when buying something new is not 'will it flatter my body' but 'will it hide my body'? If it won't, I don't buy it; it's as simple as that."

I always buy clothes much larger than I am because I don't want them even to skim my bulges; I want them to hang over the top, not touching any lumps or bumps.

My clothes disguise my non-attributes rather than drawing any attention to my attributes. I try to explain this to Juan, and he brings his legs back over one another until they are all knotted up again, shaking his head as he does so.

"You're going to be online dating; you're going to be meeting new men who need to see how gorgeous you are. They don't want to see a woman's head on top of a tent.

"OK," I say.

"So it's time to go shopping?"

"Yes," I reply.

A short bus ride later, we are speed walking through Kingston; Juan Pedro is striding ahead. I notice his shoes clickety-clack like a tap dancer as he walks; I shuffle behind in my large T-shirt and baggy tracksuit bottoms. I did my hair and makeup this morning before leaving for breakfast, but I haven't shaved my legs for God knows how long, and I'm not looking forward to parading around a shop with my fat arse and hairy legs for all to see.

As we pass Marks & Spencer's, I run to catch up with Juan. "There are clothes in here that I can fit into," I say.

He looks disdainfully at the shop window and then at me. "We can do better," he says.

"But the shop has my sizes in. You're being kind, taking me shopping, but most shops don't have clothes to fit me."

"What about this one?" says Juan, storming into little independent stores full of frilly, lacey clothing that would struggle to wrap itself around someone half my size. I've not sure I'd get the waist of some of these dresses around my wrist.

"Darling," he says, storming up to the assistant and complimenting her on her jewellery. "Wonderful, magnificent," he is saying." Now, I want you to dress my beautiful friend here in the most gorgeous clothing you have...clothing that will make her look like a desirable siren?"

"Okay," says the woman, looking bewildered at the

forceful nature of Juan and slightly dubious about the task ahead of her.

"Can I check what size you are?" she says, moving towards the rails and flicking through the clothing whilst she must know, beyond any doubt, that she has nothing there that will fit me.

"I'm about 16 to 18," I say. "Do you have clothes that big?"

"Of course they do," says Juan. "It would be madness if I didn't. They have to be able to dress people, don't they?" He looks expectantly at the woman who has not looked up from where she is frantically searching through the rails.

"You could try this 12?" she says. "These are quite generous."

Quite generous? I look at the flimsy item in her hand and at Juan.

"Try it on," he urges.

"Juan, it's at least four sizes too small."

He sighs deeply and looks at the shop assistant. "Why are you giving us clothes that don't fit her?" he asks.

"We don't have any clothes in your friend's size," she says.

"Why? Do you think my friend is fat?" he asks.

I feel my cheeks flush with colour.

"No," says the assistant, now squirming with embarrassment. "No, no, not at all."

"Then why do none of your clothes fit her? Is this a children's shop?"

"No sir," replies the assistant.

"Then it is simply a bad shop, no?"

"Well, it just caters for the slimmer lady."

"It caters for people who don't eat?"

"Yes," says the assistant. I have to say, I'm feeling quite sorry for her by now.

"Then, you should be based in Africa, yes? It would be best if you were somewhere where there are poor people who cannot afford to eat. They would welcome your services, no? Let's move this shop to where they need tiny clothes because they have no food; they have to walk 10 miles daily for water and live in poverty."

The assistant looks at him blankly.

"Or you would like to stay here?" he offers.

She nods.

"You want to stay here, in this country?"

"Yes," she says.

"Then make clothing for the people who live here. Make clothes for real people: people who have money to eat and enjoy dining out with friends, people who have lives and families, and babies. People who have real lives."

"OK," she says.

"Good," says Juan, spinning and heading out of the shop. He pauses by the rack of size zero dresses and turns back for one final assault.

"This is absurd," he says, holding the item in the air. "Any woman who starves to fit into this needs to have her head examined. These clothes are for ugly people, soulless, sad and desperate people whose hopes and dreams can be bottled, bagged, and hung in their wardrobes. Tragic."

Then, we're off, stomping out of there while a red-faced assistant watches us go.

"You're the best," I say to him when we're out on the street. "Just - the best."

"I know," he says, hugging me. "Shall we go back to that Mark and Spencing place, or whatever it was called?"

"Yep," I reply.

I swear to God, every woman needs a Juan.

DIRE WARNINGS FROM
DOWNSTAIRS DAVE

*D*ave arrives bang on the dot at 6 pm, clutching a
clipboard like he's come to do a mortgage evalua-
tion of the property or measure up for double-glazing or
something.

"Evening," he says, striding into the sitting room to greet
Charlie and Juan.

"Good God Alive," says Juan, practically swooning. "Who
in the name of all the angels in heaven are you?"

"I'm Dave. I live downstairs," he says.

"Why you're beautiful."

"Er...thank you," he says. He's gone a very bright red and
looks nervous.

"And look at you being all professional with your clipboard and smart trousers."

"I've come from work," he says defensively. "Unlike you, I
can't go to work in peacock feather trousers and a silk
blouse.

"Then you're in the wrong job," says Juan, "because you
would look completely spectacular in these trousers."

Dave gives Juan a look which forces him to recoil and

166

move to the far side of the room while I hand Dave a beer and tell him to ignore Juan. It's quite a strange moment - protecting Dave from the predatory Juan when Dave is the ultimate predator.

I explain that Charlie and Juan have arranged a pile of dates, and I will go on them without really knowing who I will meet.

"I guess it will be fun," I say without much conviction.

"Do you have lots of nice things to wear?"

"Yes," I reply. "I've got a great cream shift dress, lovely high-heel, black boots, black trousers that don't make me look like a horse and a frilly blouse. Oh, and also – a lovely, elegant cream jumper and lots of pearl necklaces that make me look like Madonna circa 1986. It should be good fun. I'm quite into the idea of internet dating now."

"You've just got to make sure you're safe – that's the most important thing," he says. "Yes – so tell me about all the dangers lurking out there."

"It's not so much that it's all desperately dangerous or anything; it's just that it's a very different way of dating, and people can act differently. You need to be aware of what could happen."

"OK, fire away then."

"Let's start with 'stashing'," he says, warming to his theme. "Ever heard of that?"

None of us has.

"OK, this is very common in internet dating...it's when you've been seeing someone, but they also see other people, so they try to keep you at arm's length...they never make you 'official'. You'll realise that they haven't introduced you to any of their friends and family - it's like they are keeping you in a box, stashing you away. This allows them to keep their options open and date other people if they want to. They haven't made you 'official' - they are having their cake and eating it. The relationship is unlikely to work, so if you meet someone like this, who does this to you - you must do the same - date lots of different people, not just the one guy. OK?"

"OK," I say. "But - I'm not wild about dating one new person, let alone a whole load."

"Treat them like they treat you, honey," says Charlie.

"OK," I say, sounding and feeling very unsure. Dating's hard. How do you know whether you're being 'stashed'?"

"What's troubling you?" asks Juan. "You've gone all quiet."

"Just the whole dating thing," I say. "It's so hard. How do you know what a guy's doing?"

"You have me here to explain," says Dave.

"No, I mean - what if a guy's being cautious and taking it slowly because he likes me and doesn't want to move too fast? I could easily mistake his intentions and think I'm being stashed."

"No - honey, you'll know. You'll feel it. You have to go with your gut instincts on these things. It only applies when you've got into a relationship, but it's worth looking out for. It's different from ghosting; in fact, it's the opposite of that - at least a ghost goes and lets you get on with your life."

"I've heard of ghosting, but not sure what it is…."

"It's one of the most well-known dating terms out there. It just means that someone you've been seeing, or talking to for a while, suddenly disappears and stops contacting you.

"It happens all the time in the gay community," says Juan. "All the time. Drives me nuts. Smile, shag, ghost. Start again. No relationships."

"Yeah, it's horrible," says Charlie. "Instead of having a break-up conversation with you, the guy you're seeing vanishes without a trace. You could have been dating someone for a few days or months, but one day they disappear. They don't return your texts and may even block you. It's cowardly."

"Then, one day, they might suddenly come back. They've been off and dated some other poor sod, then realise they like you after all, so they pop up on your phone months later. It's called Zombie-ing - when someone who dismissed you rises from the dead and comes back at you. They often act as if nothing happened. An innocuous "hey" might appear on WhatsApp or something similar to tempt you to reply.

Thanks to social media, the zombie might also try to get back into your life by following you and liking your posts on Instagram and Twitter. Even if you like the guy and want to get back with him, you have to say 'no' to Zombies, or they will do it again."

"OK, so that's ghosts and zombies. Are there any others? And do you want another beer?"

"Loads," replies Dave.

"Loads more dating advice or loads more beer?"

"Both," he says before launching into an explanation of 'benched'.

"OK, this is a bit like the sports team where you're not the first choice but left on the bench as a reserve. You find yourself being someone's backup option as they continue to look around for their ideal woman. They may come back to you if nobody better comes along, but that doesn't give one high hopes for the relationship, does it?"

"No," I say. I've got myself a pen and paper now because I feel I ought to be writing all this down.

"There's catch and release as well," says Dave. "This is what people who love the thrill of the chase do. They'll put all their effort into flirtatious texts and trying to date you until they "catch" you. But once they've caught you, they lose interest and look for someone else to chase.

"Then I should also mention breadcrumbing - when

somebody seems to be pursuing you, but really, they have no intention of being tied down to a relationship. They send you nice texts and friendly messages, like breadcrumbs, to keep you interested in them, but they're not interested. Next, there's catfishing – I mentioned this before – it's when someone lies about who they are, so they could use a completely wrong photo and give you the wrong job, age, or height. It's just when people lie about who they are...because they can. This is the internet."

"And what about kitten fishing? Is that the same sort of thing?"

"Yes – it's when you present yourself in an unrealistically positive way on your dating site – like a photo that's out of date or edited or lying about your age."

"I see. But aren't you just going to find out that they are lying as soon as you meet them?"

"Yep, which is why some of these guys won't want to meet you."

"Gosh – this sounds terrifying. Any more?"

"Well – yes – there's a slow fade, cuffing season and pulling pig...."

"I think that's enough, to be honest," Juan interrupts. I don't think we need to put her off completely."

"OK, but she was interested."

"Yeah, and that's enough."

FIRST DATE: DARREN

*H*ere we go, then, date number one, and I couldn't be happier. That's a lie; I could be much happier if I was left alone and could sit in front of the telly, drinking wine and eating pizza while feeling miserable about Ted. But I can't do that. Instead, I'm off out on a date.

"Bye, have a lovely time," shout Charlie and Juan through the living room window as I walk down the steps and out through the gate.

"Bye," says Dave, coming out of his flat and waving at me. I feel like I'm in Ballymorry or something. "Remember everything I've taught you," he adds.

"Sure," I say, speeding up as I walk towards the bus stop.

I feel a bit trussed up, to be honest. I'm in higher shoes than I'd normally wear, and the new cream dress with the pile of pearl necklaces. I can see, objectively, when I look in the mirror, that it's a good look; if anyone else were wearing it, I'd think they looked very nice. But it's not me. Not at all.

When the bus comes, I climb aboard, take a seat, and hastily remove my necklaces, shoving them into my handbag. I feel better already. Then I pull out the piece of paper they've given me with all the details of the guy I'm going to see. He's single, having been married in the past, and works for the Postal Service, which I guess means he's a postman. That's OK. That's a proper, solid, down-to-earth job. Someone you can rely on. It's a job I understand, unlike all these people who say they work in "data marketing" and "digital development". What is that? What on earth does all that mean?

"I'm vice president of crockery cleanliness."

No, mate, you wash the dishes.

Anyway, the point is that Darren is straightforward... He's a postman, and he is looking to find someone to fall in love with. Yay.

In his picture, he doesn't look like the most handsome man who ever walked the Earth, but then I'm no Beyoncé either, so that's fine. He looks friendly and approachable and as if he'd be good, fun and reliable. What more could a woman ask for?

As the bus trundles along, I fantasise to myself that this could be the one. He might be the man I've been waiting all my life to meet. Then I can cancel all those other online dates and get to know him. He can come to my house once he's finished his postal round, and we can eat pizza (most of my fantasies involve pizza). It will be perfect.

We are meeting at the Coach and Horses, the lovely pub on the green in Esher, so it's not too far for me to go and easy enough for me to get back from if he turns out not to be my Prince Charming after all. I pull out my compact and touch up my makeup, fiddling with my hair to see whether I can make it look any better without making it look too 'fussed with'

Then - we are here. I step cautiously off the bus in high heels and clip-clop towards the pub. I feel nice. I feel like a girl going on a date; I allow my anxieties and nervousness to give way to excitement. I push open the door and walk towards the bar. I see him immediately, and he clocks me immediately, standing up and coming over to introduce himself. There is an embarrassing moment where he goes in for a kiss, and I go to put my hand out and shake his, and I almost stab him in the stomach. But it's all OK, and at least I don't have to wander around the bar asking everyone whether they are Darren.

He buys me a drink, and we head to a far table to get to know one another.

First impressions are good. He is a little older than he looks in his pictures, but that's okay. He looks more or less as I expected him to. He's wearing a white shirt and cream chinos and throws his navy jumper over the back of his chair. He hands me my white wine and soda and smiles as I put it on the table.

"Thank you," I say, and he lifts his glass to toast me.

"Lovely to meet you," he says, and we touch our glasses lightly together. He smiles again. He has good teeth. He doesn't have very nice eyes, though. This is a bit of a shame because I always think that nice eyes are a sign of a nice guy.

"So, tell me a little bit about yourself," he says… And, we are off… We are doing the Internet dating thing, revealing details about ourselves which will help us work out whether we want to spend time together, trying to work out whether there's a spark, trying to find areas of mutual interest.

The conversation flows nicely between us, with him chatting away, and we're discovering lots of mutual interests and people we think we might have in common. He lives in Esher, where my mum and dad live; I'm not far away in Cobham. He's been to the DIY and gardening shop where I work and tells me what fun it was there at Christmas. I was the one put in charge of Christmas, so I feel a warm glow of appreciation at this comment.

"So, what's your dating history then?" I say, and he tells me that his most recent girlfriend dumped him just a couple of weeks ago. He looks heartbroken as he says this, and a little red flag pops up in my mind. The first red flag, so there is nothing to be too scared about.

"Had you been seeing her long?" I ask.

"No," he says. "Not a long time, and we had only been on a handful of dates, but when she disappeared suddenly without contacting me, it brought back all sorts of terrible memories...."

Ah, I think to myself, ghosting. I remember Juan telling me about that. (I don't share the news with Darren that this is very common in Internet dating, though).

"The memories..." Darren is saying.

"Is everything alright?" I ask. I'm unsure whether I'm supposed to ask for more details about his personal life or let him sit there, drifting back into memories.

"My wife died ten years ago," he says. "She was the love of my life; I adored her. She was everything to me. I hadn't dated since her death; I concentrated on bringing up our daughter, then I decided to make room for dating, and I went out and met Marissa, but then she just disappeared. No explanation, no word about why she didn't want to see me again. Just gone.

"The whole incident has brought back the pain of losing my wife. It's been a tricky couple of weeks, to be honest."

"Goodness," I say. "Losing your wife like that must've been terrible."

"It was horrific," he says. "She was a teacher at a local junior school, and after we had our baby - Susie - she went in to show the teachers our new little girl. When she walked out, pushing our baby in a pushchair, a motorbike swerved off the road, crashed into her and killed her. He missed Susie by inches."

"Gosh," I say, my hand flying up to my mouth and my eyes wide in disbelief. "That must've been awful."

"She was in a coma for a week; then I had to switch off the machine," he says. Awful doesn't begin to cover it.

"I'm so, so sorry," I keep repeating, in the absence of words that better sum up how I'm feeling. What do you say to a stranger when he starts revealing this sort of thing to you?

"Do you mind if we head back soon?" he says after a short silence. "I like you, but I'm afraid I will not give a very good account of myself. I'll get more and more upset if we stay here like this. Maybe I can see you again when I'm not feeling so awful?"

"Of course, that's no problem at all," I say, reaching for my bag. "There is a bus due in five minutes; I'll head off now and jump on it."

"No," says Darren. "I wouldn't hear of it. Please, you're about five minutes away; let me drop you at home; it's the least I can do."

"If you're sure," I say.

"I'm absolutely sure," he says, standing up. "I'm very sorry about tonight...I don't know why I suddenly got so maudlin. I'm normally quite good company, or so I'm told."

"Please don't worry, it's not a problem at all," I say as I follow him outside and climb into his car next to him.

"I'm sorry again about tonight. You must think me a fool," he says.

In truth, I'm not at all bothered about tonight. He seems like a nice chap, but there was certainly no spark between us, and he's got a long way to go to start feeling better about himself again before he can date anyone properly.

He pulls out from the curb and drives towards the end of the road, approaching a roundabout at which he has to turn left. But he indicates right and goes all the way round the roundabout. I suddenly have a panic in the pit of my stomach. Why is he not taking me home? I've given him my address; he knows this is the wrong way.

"This isn't the way to go," I say, slightly nervously.

"Yes, I know," he says. "Will you bear with me? There's something I want to show you."

"Of course," I say. "Will it take very long?"

"Nope, we're just here," he says, pulling over to the side of the road and putting on his hazard warning lights. "Here," he says.

Here?" I repeat. "Why have you brought me here."

"This is where she was hit by the motorcycle. Right here, in that spot. Her body was lying across the road there. There was blood everywhere. The ambulance and police cars came that way and parked there. I ran over and tried to hold her and talk to her. I lay next to her and was covered in her blood. The blood was everywhere. Then they took her to hospital."

I look at him. I don't know what to say or do. He is staring at the road, but in his mind, he is back ten years when his life suddenly spun off its axis.

"I'd like to go home now," I say, and he drives off, taking me home without either of us saying another word.

SECOND DATE: STUART

*J*uan and Charlie sit on the sofa in stunned silence while Dave paces around the room, punching his fist into his hand.

"What a dick," he says.

"No, no, he's not a dick. He's just still grieving. His girl-friend's disappearance brought back all the memories of losing his wife."

"I don't care how upset he was; you don't take someone on a first date to see where a motorbike crushed your wife," says Dave. "And without telling you. If he'd said that he wanted to visit the place where his wife died, would you like to come? You could have said, 'no thanks, you giant weirdo, I want to go home'. But not to ask you and to assume that you might want to go. On a first date. The man's a freak."

"We are coming with you tomorrow night," said Charlie. "We will sit either in a nearby pub so you can reach us in an emergency or in the pub itself."

"No, that's crazy. There's no need. Look, I've made this guy sound odder than he was. He was nice."

"NO," says Dave. "No, no. He was odd. He showed you

where the blood splatters were on the road when his wife was killed. If you don't think that's odd and very inappropriate, you need to have much higher standards."

"And where are your necklaces?" asks Juan. "Did he steal your necklaces?"

"What?" says Dave. "He stole from you?"

"No, he did nothing of the kind. They are in my bag. I'm fine. Please - all of you, stop making this into a drama. I'm going to bed.

"IT IS A DRAMA," they all call after me.

The next day I'm up early and off to work, leaving Juan in the flat. Charlie's also at work today, so he's all alone, and God only knows what mischief he'll get up to. I've told him he must not go down and bother Dave all day.

"I won't," he said.

"You won't accidentally get locked out wearing nothing but a pink G-string?"

"Ooooo...stop putting ideas in my mind."

"Juan!"

"No, I promise I won't."

"OK then."

In the end, he seems to have spent most of the day staking out the pub I'm meeting tonight's date in and working out where he and Charlie could place themselves out of sight but able to pounce if the date goes wrong. By the time I return that evening, he's planned it like a military invasion.

He has a detailed map of the pub garden printed out.

"We will enter from this direction," he says, showing me red arrows drawn onto the map, and this is the likely rendezvous point." He shows a squiggle that he's drawn next to the bar. "So, you two will probably sit here...." There's another squiggle drawn at a table near the bar.

"Perfect," I say. "Now I'm going to get changed because I'm meeting him in an hour."

"I've laid out your clothes on your bed," says Juan.

"What? Am I not allowed to make any decisions myself?"

"None," says Juan.

I go into my room to see that, happily, he's put out black trousers and high boots for tonight. It's chillier this evening than yesterday, and it's bound to get cold as the evening goes on, especially if we're outside. I put away the frilly top that he made me buy and pull out a loose-fitting cream jumper that I like and which fits me (the frilly blouse strains across my chest, which Juan seems to think is a good thing, but I most definitely do not).

I emerge from the room and stand there to be inspected.

"More make-up," insists Juan, sending me back to my room to put on the brightest lipstick I own. I come back out and am greeted by a frown.

"This is it," I say. "This is as much makeup as I can bear to put on."

"What about the frilly blouse?"

I tell him I'm wearing it under the jumper (a damned lie), and we head for the pub. When we arrive, Juan tells me to act normally - as if the two of them weren't there - and they will leap into action if things get difficult.

This scenario has huge comedy potential, though I don't mention that. The thought of Charlie and Juan leaping into action and beating up a badly-behaved suitor is lovely. Together they weigh less than I do. I can't imagine Charlie ever fighting with anyone, she is the most gentle and lovely person ever, and I don't imagine Juan is a secret Mike Tyson - though he was awesome in that dress shop.

I go into the pub to get myself a glass of wine from the bar, then head back outside, sitting down at the loveliest table I can find, one that allows me to catch the last of the day's rays while being able to see Charlie and Juan on the other side of the beer garden. Juan is waving wildly. I thought they were supposed to be undercover over there. Charlie nudges him as if reading my mind, and he lowers his hands slowly.

I take a large sip and sit back in my chair. I can't work out whether to wear my sunglasses or not. I'm never sure whether they make me look mysterious and elegant or simply unapproachable and daft.

I'm doing the ridiculous, off, on again with the glasses, when a man appears in the garden and looks around. He fits the brief given to me by Charlie and Juan but doesn't seem to be coming over to me. When I look over at them, they are smiling and putting the thumbs up; this is clearly him. He is a nice-looking man, stocky but not fat, quite big and manly looking. Very attractive. I pull the sunglasses off and smile over at him. He stops and his tracks and looks back. Then he walks into the bar, clearly not recognising that it's me. What do I do now? Run after him? I decide to sit there for a couple of minutes while he gets his drink, and he might wander back out again when he sees I'm not in the bar. So, I sit back, take another gulp of wine, and smile over at Charlie.

Just as I'm relaxing, a sudden shadow is cast over me, and I look up to see the man who was in the garden earlier.

"Ah, hello. You must be Stuart?" I say, standing up. He's very attractive close-up. "I'm Mary."

"Oh, it is you...I wasn't sure," he mutters, taking two enormous gulps of his drink.

"I know, it's hard. When you don't quite know who you're looking for. Nice to meet you."

I put out my hand, and he looks at it as if I've pulled a knife on him. He's just staring at it. Then he takes another huge gulp of his drink and plonks his glass down heavily on the table, causing the small metal table to shake a little on the unsteady ground and some of the beer to splash out of the top and onto my cream jumper.

"Look, I can't do this," he says. "I'm sorry. I'm sure you're lovely. But this isn't going to work for me" Then he backs away, leaving me standing there with splashes of beer on my jumper. I see Charlie and Juan getting to their feet.

"I'm sorry...you're fatter than I thought you'd be. I'm sorry. That sounds rude, but you're too fat for me. I am very, very sorry."

By now, Juan has reached us.

"Sorry?" he says. "You're 'very, very sorry? You dog."

Stuart looks alarmed by the arrival of Juan and the lecture he's getting, so he runs. I've never seen anything like it. He's sprinting off through the garden towards the carpark as if lions are chasing him. Then Juan runs after him, hurling expletives in Spanish.

"Eres horrible, feo, cerdo," he cries.

"Cómo puedes tratar a mi amigo así?"

Charlie and I watch him go. We have no idea what he's shouting, but we know it's not pleasant.

"Mary es bella," he shouts at Stuart's retreating. "Mary es bella."

Then he turns around and walks back to us. "Pig," he says. "You are too good for this little pig."

We look from one to the other before Juan gives me a big hug. "Who does he think he is? Running away like that. Does he think he's Usain Bolt or something? Pig. Now, we get drunk." Juan leads me to the bar, with Charlie in hot pursuit. "Now we get very drunk and forget all about Dead Wife Darren last night and Usain Bolt this night. There are better men to come, Mary. I promise you; better men are out there."

After that, we did drink a lot, to be fair – we consumed vast amounts of alcohol, but I did that thing where I felt more and more sober the more I drank. I wasn't desperately unhappy or anything. Surprisingly it didn't bother me what the guy had said. This dating lark showed me that I'm much more resilient than I ever thought I was. Usain Bolt could say what he wanted. I know I'm fat, for God's sake. Does he think I don't have mirrors? And I'd love to lose weight, but right now, I'm this weight, and if the fact that I like cake is such a deal breaker for him, then we probably weren't going to get on anyway. The only thing I did feel slightly miserable about was that every failed dating experience made me think about Ted and how amazingly perfect he was. I thought I would spend the rest of my life with Ted. It made me so sad that I wasn't and was now on dates with all these strange guys. Why the hell had it all gone wrong with Ted? Perhaps I should call him and make it up to him?

"Hi," says a slurred voice as I sit there, phone in hand, wondering whether to call.

"Hello," I reply. "I'm not very good company at the moment."

"I'll be the judge of that," he says, dropping into a seat next to me and raising his glass. I lift mine, too and gently clink it against his.

"I saw what happened," he says. "Earlier. You know - the idiot running off."

"Yeah - that wasn't great," I reply.

"He's a dick."

"No - I think you'll find he's a pig," I reply, and we both collapse into laughter.

"Yes. The sight of your friend running after him, screaming at him in a foreign language, made my night."

"At least it turned a nasty moment into a very funny one."

"Don't think of it as a nasty evening," says Harry. "Think of him as a nasty person, but also think of the lovely friends who stood up for you and think of me - someone who has met you and likes you."

"You like me? But you don't know me."

"I've been listening to you and your friends talk. You seem lovely."

"Thank you," I say.

Would you come out for a drink with me one night to get to know one another better?"

"Really?"

"Yes. Will you come out with me? Maybe tomorrow night?"

"I'm not sure whether I'm free tomorrow," I say. "Can I text you and let you know?"

"Of course," he says, putting his number into my phone. "Text me when you know what night you've got free."

"I will," I say, and smile at how funny it is that I have to find out from my diary of dates when I can fit him in before we can make any plans. I may be on the wrong side of 25 and several stones overweight, but this dating lark might turn out OK after all.

Later that night, I sit next to Charlie while she looks through the timetable she's drawn up.

"You know this is going to cause all sorts of administrative problems for me, don't you?" she says, as she deploys pencils, rubbers and rulers to her rather complicated-looking chart. "I'll have to go back to the timetable and adjust everyone, and we'll have to take someone out if you want to add the new guy in."

"And wouldn't it be funny," I say. "If after all the work you've done to try and introduce me to new men, I find someone I bumped into myself."

"Funny? I can think of other words for it – like bloody annoying," says Charlie.

"You love me, really," I say, reaching over to hug her but

stumbling into her and almost flattening her. Perhaps I'm drunker than I realised.

"I love you too," she says, her voice coming up from somewhere beneath me.

"Now, get off me, and let me see whether I can make this work."

Once she's upright, she looks at her plans. "We drop the drippy one we weren't sure about and slot Harry in."

"Perfect," I say. "Now, I better go to bed."

THIRD DATE: MARTIN

$\mathcal{I}$ feel quite conspicuous walking up the street towards the Post Office at 5.30 pm to meet tonight's date. It's quite an old place to meet someone - the post office -and this is so early. But he insists that there's a lovely cafe nearby that we can go to and that earlier is better. Charlie and Juan have parked in the pub opposite the Post Office, so they are nearby in case anything happens. After last night's runaway date, Juan is keener than ever to ensure that he is nearby in case of any problems. I've let them come tonight, but I'm going to stop them from coming to the rest of the dates, or it will get crazy.

As I approach the meeting point, I can see that he's not there yet - there is just a guy with his young kid looking at all the postcards in the window. So, I stop at the furniture shop next door, which has a big mirror in the window and adjust my hair. I am pouting, preening, and double-checking that there is no lipstick on my teeth when I feel a gentle tap on my shoulder.

"Are you Mary?" says the guy with the young boy.

"Yes."

"I'm Martin," he says. Lovely to meet you." He puts his hand out to shake mine rather formally. This is so weird. Why's he got a kid with him?

"Can I introduce Matt?"

Matt is about five years old and looks like he'd rather be anywhere else on Earth than meet me.

"Hello, Matt," I say as the little boy looks at the ground and digs his hands in his pocket.

"Don't be rude; shake the nice lady's hand," says Martin. Matt looks at me from beneath a floppy fringe and sneers a little.

"Don't worry," I say quickly. "It's lovely to meet you, Matt."

"I hope you didn't mind meeting at the Post Office; it seemed the easiest place. We could go to the cafe at the end of the road for a bite. They do half-price kids' meals on Thursdays."

"Sure," I say. I'm not quite sure whether this is some joke. I don't mean to be rude, and it must be hard to find babysitters, but who in god's name brings their child on a date with them?

We head to the cafe at the corner of the road, with Martin spending the whole time telling Matt to stop fiddling with his hair and to put away his electronic game. Matt doesn't utter a sound, not even a grunt, the whole time I'm there. We get to the cafe, and Martin goes in first and orders a table for two before adding quickly;

"Oh no, sorry, no – a table for three. Sorry, I forgot Mary was with us."

Forgot Mary was with us. Forgot Mary was with us. This is supposed to be a date that I'm on.

We sit at our table next to many other tables, forming a circle around a play area in the middle. Matt rushes into the play area and shrieks along with the other children as they do that game you find in every doctor's waiting room, where you have to slide the coloured balls around twisting metal poles.

I look down at the table with its grubby Formica table-cloth. There are crayons and paper on it for the children and a 'design a hat' competition. Martin smiles at the adults there; they are parents at Matt's school. It was bad enough when I thought he'd brought Matt on our date, but now I realise he's taking me on his evening out with Matt. This is crackers. He chats to the other parents who are there (mainly mums) but doesn't introduce me, so I sit in silence while they discuss some forthcoming school trips.

"AI used to love school trips when I was little," I say. "They were always good fun."

"Do you have children?" asks one of the mothers sitting opposite.

"No, I don't," I say, and they all turn back and continue doing what they were doing.

This is ridiculous. I'm not quite sure what to do or what to say. Should I walk out? But then the waitress arrives and takes our order. I order orange squash, fish fingers and chips because that's what everyone else is ordering. Then I head off to the toilets and sink heavily on the seat, pulling my phone out to text Juan.

"Reinforcements required. I seem to be on a play date with a bunch of five-year-olds. I'm at the dinosaur café on the High Street. Please help!"

I look at myself in the mirror, all dressed up, with hair freshly styled and wearing my new earrings and favourite lipstick. I look better than I have for ages, all to sit in a cafe with a bunch of children.

Back in the café, I discover a skinny little boy has climbed into my seat.

"Do you want to play action man with me?" he asks.

187

"Of course she does," says Martin. He turns to me: "You'd like that, wouldn't you?"

My phone bleeps in my bag, and I pray with all my might that it's Juan confirming they are on their way.

I pick up a broken action man and dress him as a soldier while other children gather around and join in the fun.

I put my phone down on the table. "Will be there in two minutes," it says.

Thank God for that.

I'm just marching a one-legged Action Man into war when the little bell on the door rings, and the extravagant Juan and gorgeous Charlie walk into the café and stop, open-mouthed, as they see me and three 5-year-olds playing wargames with action men.

"What on earth?" says Charlie as a little boy called Freddie tells me to surrender.

Juan says something in Spanish which probably wouldn't bear translating in front of all the children, and I shrug my shoulders.

"You've beaten me," I say to Freddie. "Now you're king of all the world."

"That's not how it works," replies Freddie. "You don't become King of all the world just because you win a fight."

"Well, you should," I say. "You should be King Freddie."

"Yay!" he shouts, overjoyed.

Then I turn to Martin. "I'm afraid I have to go; something's come up," I say as I stand and bid farewell to everyone.

"Oh no, you're not going, are you? I like you a lot. Please stay," comes a voice. But it's not the voice of Martin, who couldn't give a toss whether I'm there or not; it's the voice of Freddie, the little boy I've been playing action man with.

"I'm so sorry," I say. "But I have to go to work now. I'll tell you what – you can have my fish fingers when they come."

"Yum!" says the boy. And I head towards the door while all the parents look at me in complete confusion. They don't know why I came and have no idea why I'm suddenly leaving.

Just as I'm almost through the door, little Freddie comes charging towards me and grabs my legs, begging me to stay. "Shoo, shoo," says Juan, attempting to move the kid from me in the way one might dispense pigeons landing on the table.

"Shoo, shoo," he repeats.

Eventually, one of the mothers comes over and takes her son back. He burst into tears when he sees I'm going. Martin, meanwhile, doesn't seem to have looked up from his colouring book.

BALLS ON SHOW

*I*t's my date with Harry today, and I was planning to spend the day relaxing and beautifying myself so I look as good as possible, but the sound of a commotion outside the window wakes me up. Raised voices and a car revving maniacally outside wrest me from my slumber. What the hell on earth is going on out there? I pull back the curtains and peer through. I see Dawn below standing by her car, hands on hips, while a guy sits in the driver's seat revving it.

Shit, I completely forgot that Dawn was coming today. I jump away from the window, pull the curtains closed and run around getting myself dressed and looking half decent. I rush into the living room where Juan Pedro is standing, one leg extended behind him in an arabesque.

"Morning, darling, just doing my wake-up exercises," he says before swinging his leg around and holding it out in front in such an elegant way. He is a delight to watch… Such a sophisticated mover. I have no idea how he manages to swing his legs around the way he does.

"I think Dawn is here," he says. "But I'm staying away

because it sounds like they're having car trouble, and I'm getting very aggressive out there. Cars and aggression or two things I don't do."

"Yes, I heard all the shouting and the engine revving… I suppose I better go out and check everything is okay."

Juan brings his leg down to the floor elegantly and turns with a flourish to follow me out of the flat. "I'm coming as backup," he says. "But I'm not touching any engines…or big oily ends."

We get outside to hear Dawn bellowing at her boyfriend, Steve. He is a rough-looking chap with more tattoos than hair and a gruff voice that can only be earned by regularly inhaling smoke. The man must be on about 80 cigarettes a day.

"Darling Mary, how are you?" says Dawn when she sees me, dropping her argument with Simon as she moves to embrace me.

"Let me introduce Juan," I say, indicating Juan standing next to me. Dawn's eyes open wide as she takes in his attire… Very baggy harem trousers that make him look a bit like Aladdin and a tight gold T-shirt. It's funny, I get used to how Juan dresses, so it doesn't surprise me to see him looking like someone in a pantomime. But other people's looks remind me he is a very original dresser.

"I'm going to have to go under the car, love," says Steve. He steps out of the car… He is wearing quite small shorts for a large man, and I must stop my gaze from dropping to his shorts area.

"Nice to see you," I say. "My name is Mary."

"Steve," he says, kissing me on the cheek, then turns to look Juan up and down. "You must be Ted," he says.

"I'm Juan," he says quickly, "I'm a friend of Mary."

Let's get this thing up in the air and have a look at what's going on, shall we," he says, taking a jack out of the boot and beginning to lift the front of the car. He messes around for a while, stabilising it, then comes to the front and eases himself underneath it until just his legs and shorts stick out.

"Have you got a torch?" he says. "And maybe some rags or something?"

"Sure, I'll go and look now," I say, heading back into my flat. Dawn follows me, and we rummage around until we have found everything he needs. Then we head back outside. Dawn reaches down to hand the rags to Steve, with me by her side. But as she reaches in with the rags, she sees that he's popped out of his shorts.

I see it, too, and it's a most alarming sight.

"Oh my God," she says, dropping the rags and leaning over to tuck him back into his shorts. Then she pulls the shorts down a bit to ensure he doesn't escape again, cupping him to ensure he's all tucked up inside. Then she pushes the rags and the torch underneath the car and stands up. I stand next to her. Standing next to us is...Steve. What?

"Who the hell is under that car?" says Dawn. We both look down at the pavement at the man she's just fondled. Then the man pushes himself back, and Dave emerges.

"What the hell was that?" he says.

"I thought you were my boyfriend," says Dawn.

"No. No, I'm not," he replies.

"Dave came out and offered to help, so he is sorting out the oil leak," says Juan. Steve says nothing... He stares at Dawn like he can't believe what she just did. None of us can quite believe what she did just did. Dave has turned the brightest pink imaginable and won't meet anyone's eyes.

After the car gate disaster, Dawn and Martin come inside, and we have a cup of tea and chat amiably without anyone mentioning what Dawn just did.

"The reason I wanted to come and see you," she says. "Is

that I've got another trip for you, if you fancy going on it… a trip to St Lucia."

"Oh my God," I say. "Is it for the blog?"

Dawn runs a blog called "two fat ladies" about larger ladies going on various adventures and reporting back. I've been on a safari for her and a cruise, which was great fun though full of slip-ups and disasters. St Lucia, though. Blimey, that sounds like the most incredible trip in the world.

"Oh my God, I'd love that so much," I say.

"You can take someone," says Dawn. "If there are any hot men in your life right now, tell them they can come to St Lucia with you. If not, take a friend. You have to remember to report back on the blog four times a day and send videos and pictures."

"Yes, that's not a problem," I say, thinking of a dreamy island in the Caribbean and how amazing that would be.

"Thanks so much, Dawn," I say. "That's brilliant."

FOURTH DATE: HARRY

I am still buzzing when I prepare to head out that evening to meet Harry. My plans to spend the day relaxing and beautifying were blown to smithereens by the news that I could be heading off to St Lucia. I mean - St Lucia! Have you seen that place? It's all turquoise oceans and beaches fringed with palm trees, white sands and boats with white sails. I've never seen anywhere so beautiful before.

"It might be the loveliest place I've ever seen," said Charlie, sounding choked and close to tears, as she looked at pictures of the place on her phone.

"I know," I replied, and then we fell into a respectful silence as we looked at the pictures together.

The sudden ringing of the phone broke us out of our reverie. It was Harry.

"Hello."

"It's Harry here. You're going to hate me."

"Am I?"

"Yes, look, I can't make it tonight."

"Great," I reply before I can stop myself.

"I'm sorry," he says.

"Don't worry. It's better than you coming to meet me and then running away. At least you've had the decency to phone."

"It's my mum," he says. "She's ill. I'm in hospital with her."

"Oh. Gosh. Is she OK?"

"A small heart attack; she should be OK, though. I don't want to leave her."

"No, I completely understand. Go and see her, and thanks for letting me know."

I put the phone down, and there's a text straight away. It's from Dave, wishing me luck on my date.

"He's cancelled," I reply. "His mum is in hospital."

"Oh really," says Dave. "Did he suggest another date?"

"No," I say.

"Then he could be benching you."

Great. Thanks, Dave.

FIFTH DATE: RUPERT

I woke up this morning to a text from Harry asking me whether we can meet another night; of course, this has caused real trauma to Charlie, but she is making alterations to the timetable to accommodate him. I'm glad he wants to meet me. I was concerned when Dave said I was being benched. Perhaps this dating lark isn't too terrible after all.

I'm off today, so I'm going to get my nails done and my eyebrows waxed before tonight's date. That is how committed I am to this process!

I take out the dress that I have decided to wear – it's the cream one that I wore on the first date because it's loose, comfortable and makes me feel good. I'll forego the jumble of necklaces, though.

Since I will be wearing cream, I have decided to get my nails painted in a gorgeous fudge colour. I know that sounds like a horrid colour, but they look great and will look more sophisticated with a cream dress than red or bright pink would. I'm feeling quite pleased as I lay back on the bed to have my eyebrows waxed into shape.

"What sort of thing were you thinking of?" says Melody, the stylist, sizing up my eyebrows as she pushes, pulls, lifts, and separates them. "They are quite bushy. Shall I give them a whole new shape?"

"I'm not sure," I say.

"I just think it would look a bit more modern."

"I thought the rage was for bigger eyebrows?"

"Yes, but not quite this big."

"OK, fine," I say. "You do what you think is best."

Then I lay back and think of people with perfect eyebrows, like Meghan Markle and Cheryl Cole.

Two hours later…

"It's not that bad," say Juan and Charlie.

"It looks painful, though," Charlie adds. "Does it hurt?"

"Of course, it hurts," I say. "It stings and feels raw. And obviously, I look as if I've been rubbing my face up against sandpaper. This bloke I'm going on a date with tonight will think I'm a nutter."

"He might not," says Juan. "Some people are into that sort of thing. I met this guy once who said he went to a gay orgy, and one of the guys pulled out rough sandpaper…."

"Okay, okay, not helping," I cry.

I don't need to hear from Juan that the only people likely to be interested in me are those who prefer vigorous sex involving sandpaper.

"What am I going to do?"

Besides the fact that my face looks red raw in a streak along my eyebrows, there's also the fact that my eyebrows have been so overly shaped that there is hardly anything left of them, and I look peculiar.

"Did you say anything to her?" says Charlie. "You know, like tell her she stripped off your skin away and made you look ridiculous."

"No, of course, I didn't," I reply. "I'm British. I never complain about anything. I wanted to get out of there as quickly as possible and head home."

"Was it the same place you had that facial before, where you looked like you'd been boiled alive for a couple of days?"

"Er, yes," I say. I shouldn't have gone back there, but it's cheaper than everywhere else.

"Do you think I look OK, Juan?" I say.

"Well, you look like a Burns victim," he says, with a distinct lack of consideration for my feelings. "But this is what makeup was made for. We will get you fixed up and looking glorious in no time."

Half an hour later...

I don't look glorious. I should say that right at the start. I've got so much makeup on that I look like a bloody geisha girl.

"You just look perfectly made up, and as if you've made an effort," says Charlie in an attempt to reassure me.

"Yes, I've made an effort for someone who wants to be a clown."

"I didn't know what else to do," says Juan. "I thought I would put make-up on just around the eyebrows, but I didn't realise how much I have to put, and then it looked very odd with the rest of the face, so I had to put it on the rest of the face as well, and – well – this is the result."

"You look lovely; please don't worry," says Charlie.

They are both standing in the hallway, looking at me as I look at myself in the mirror. To be fair to Juan, he's done a good job. I look a lot better than I did earlier. You can't see the lightning streaks of raw red around my eyes, and my eyebrows are now back to normal. Much fuller than they were a few hours earlier, thanks to Juan's artistic flair with pencils and brushes. There's nothing wrong with what he's done; it's just that there's way too much of it. I must have half a bottle of foundation on my face.

"Just don't rub your eyebrows because they're 90% eyeliner pencil," says Juan. "Then you'll be okay."

"OK," I say. "I guess I should go…."

I have managed to persuade Charlie and Juan not to come with me on this date…it's in a small, cosy pub, and it will be obvious that they are with me.

"I'll be fine," I promise them. "I'll text you when I'm leaving."

I only know that Rupert is 42 (but he looks a lot older than that in his picture). He looks nice, and Charlie's notes on him say he is very courteous, well-spoken and quite bright and well-off, which augurs well.

We've arranged to meet at a bar near Hampton Court Palace. It's a lovely place with tables outside from which you can see the palace on one side and the river on the other side. I think it might be my favourite pub in the whole world, called the Phoenix Arms. Inside it has a Baroque feel with loads of gorgeous big velvet armchairs and sofas in wonderful jewel colours, piles of cushions and gentle music in the background. There is a small gin bar in one corner and the main bar serving all the usual drinks. Upstairs is a restaurant that offers the best views imaginable over the palace. It is called, predictably enough, 'The Henry VIII'. We arranged to meet downstairs, and he told Charlie that if I fancy dinner, we could do that afterwards.

I walk into the bar and don't see him first of all. He is tucked in the corner of the room, folded into one of the big velvet sofas. I smile as I see him clambering out of it in a very ungainly fashion - he's all knees and elbows as he staggers to his feet. As I predicted, he's much older than his photo indicated. He looks strangely familiar, though I've no idea where from. Perhaps he has one of those faces?

He has a lovely manner and bounds up to me, smiling and proffering his hand, but he also hugs and kisses me on the cheek.

"What can I get you to drink then?" he says, with an impish smile and a Bambi-ish demeanour that makes me feel unaccountably happy.

"I'd love a gin and tonic, especially if they have fruity flavours, like rhubarb. I love those."

"Oh, that sounds good; let's go to the gin bar and see what they've got."

This, I predict, it's going to be a very successful date.

He is considerably older than me, and I wouldn't say I fancied him as such, but then I didn't fancy Ted I first met him. His personality was what won me over and made me feel great.

I'm sure the same thing could happen again if I got to know this guy.

He seems lovely, and hopefully, he hasn't got any dead wives he wants to introduce me to.

We take our drinks over to two beautiful green velvet armchairs.

"I think these armchairs might be safer," he says. "He took me about 20 minutes to get out of that sofa over there. I wouldn't want to subject you to that."

I smile. I love his self-deprecating humour and warmth.

As I look at him, he does seem familiar.

"Do you live round here?" I ask him.

"Yes, I do," he says. "I live and work in the area. I do love Hampton Court."

"Me too," I say. "I don't come here anywhere near enough. Whenever I do come, I think how amazingly beautiful it is."

"We should go to the Palace for the day one time," he says, all wide-eyed and friendly. "We could tour and learn about the wives and the incredible tyrant who lived there."

"Of yes, that would be fantastic," I say. He is lovely. But I just have this odd sneaking feeling in the back of my mind that I know him from somewhere. Where could I know him from?

"So, tell me all about yourself," he says, and I talk about my job in the DIY centre, how I met Ted, and we got on brilliantly and had a lovely relationship, but it seemed to have run its course, so we have gone our separate ways. He tells me he used to be married too, but they split a long time ago, and his wife remarried. He works as a locum doctor moving between practices, but he also has a private practice which is his main focus, and he treats mainly children.

"I love it," he says. "It's very difficult treating children because they're not as good as adults are at expressing what's wrong, so you have to fiddle around and interpret what they're saying much more, but when you solve a child's problem, it is the loveliest feeling in the world."

"I bet it is," I say. "It must be great to be able to make people better."

"Yes, I'm lucky to have a job I love so much."

I notice that his glass is already empty.

"Would you like another drink?" I ask.

"No, no, let me get this," he says, reaching down to his jacket that has fallen onto the floor to pull out his wallet. He looks up at me: "Same again?"

That's when I realise where I know him from; as he looks up at me, the memory came flooding back. The last time I saw him, I had no knickers on.

"I think I know where I know you from," I say, all hesitant and flushed with embarrassment.

"Do you sometimes work as a gynaecologist?"

"Yes, I work in all areas of general practice. Is that a problem?"

"No, not a problem, but I think you worked as my gynaecologist; I came in to see you earlier in the week. I lost my knickers."

It's all too weird for words. I can't cope with this. This guy is my gynaecologist. How can I sit and have a drink with him? I feel so embarrassed, though he seems entirely unperturbed. He stands to go over to get the drinks while I drop my head into my hands, running them through my hair and across my face. Trying to calm myself down and work out what to do.

He arrives back, and his eyes almost pop out of his head.

"Your eyebrows have completely disappeared?" He says. "And you've got soot or something all over your forehead. Are you OK?"

"Oh Christ, that's my eyebrows," I say. "I was rubbing my face. Oh, never mind."

He's a lovely guy, but I can't sit here and drink with a guy who had his hand inside me just a few days ago. It's not good for me at all.

"I'm so sorry," I say. "You seem like a top man, but you're my gynaecologist. This is so weird. Do you mind if I leave?"

"Goodness, I've just bought the drinks," he says. "Are you sure?"

"Yes, perfectly sure," I say, grabbing my handbag and cardigan and going to leave. "I'm sorry. This is just making me feel so weird. I'm sorry."

I start to walk away, and he calls after me.

"I found them," he says, standing up and shouting.

"Found what?"

"Your knickers," he says. "After you left, I found your knickers under the bed."

"Oh God," I say as I turn and walk away, through the pretty bar, past the colourful sofas and the people at the bar who are now staring at me.

I can never, ever go back to that place again, and I can never, ever visit a gynaecologist again.

SIXTH DATE; HARRY (TAKE II)

"*N*oooooo..." says Juan. "The very doctor who did your girly bits? Was he the guy on the date?"

"YES!"

"Oh...it's too much!" Juan paces around the bedroom. To his credit, he's not laughing at the comic elements of this latest romantic fiasco but appears to fully understand the awfulness of what happened.

"Your date tonight will be nice. You know him, and you know he is a lovely man because he looked after his mother when she was ill, so that is good."

"You don't think he was benching me?"

"No, because now he has made a date with you. I am happy now that he is nice, decent, and normal."

"Yes, I say. "I'm looking forward to it. He's normal and hasn't seen my vagina, so it'll be a pleasant change.

Juan shudders dramatically and leaves to let me get ready.

At 6 pm, I walk into the pub and see Harry sitting there, focusing intently on the newspaper in front of him, poised with pen in hand. He's lost in thought as he studies the paper in front of him.

"Good evening," I say. "Are you struggling?"

"Yes. It's sudoku...drives me nuts. I've no idea why I put myself through it."

I take a seat opposite him, and he puts down his paper. "Don't let me forget that, will you?" he says. "I hate it if I put it down and forget to take it. These are mine, as well. There's a pile of newspapers on the floor by his feet.

"Gosh, you love your sudoku, don't you?" I say.

"Listen," he replies. "I've got a proposal for you. I could go to the bar and get us a drink here or, I don't know whether you fancy it, but I made some supper for us earlier. I didn't want to put you off by inviting you to mine, so I thought we'd meet here and see what you thought, but it's all there, waiting for us if you're hungry.

"It's just chilli con carne with rice and some cheesy garlic bread, and I've made a big salad too...and some rosemary roasted potatoes because I remember you saying before that you liked them. Do you fancy coming back for supper in the garden? I've got some wine at home, too...completely up to you. No pressure. The food won't go to waste, so only if you want to." I look at him for a moment. I know I shouldn't go back to his flat, but this is the third time I've seen him, and he does seem perfectly normal. And he likes newspapers. Men who like newspapers are usually fairly sober, straightforward and decent human beings, aren't they? And the food sounds so good.

"Sure," I say. "I'd like that."

His house is near the pub, a short stroll down a lovely, tree-lined street. I wonder how he has managed to afford one of these big, imposing houses when we turn into a side road flanked by less salubrious properties. They are still nice, but much smaller and more in keeping with what I was expecting. There's a block of flats at the far side of the cul-de-sac. "This is me," he says, opening the front door and allowing me to pass through a lovely, bright, airy reception area.

"This is lovely," I say.

"Oh, thank you," he replies. "I like it here...look - he walks me across the reception area to the huge window on the other side, which looks out onto...the river.

"Oh My God...river views!" I shriek. "I thought they were an urban myth...I didn't know they actually existed."

"Ha, ha," he replies. "Yes, we're lucky here - river views, a gym in the basement and a tennis court outside. It's a fine place."

"Wow," I say. "That does sound lovely."

"Not that I use the gym," he says. "Or the river views."

I smile at this because I don't quite know what he means. 'Don't use the river views'? How odd is that? Little do I know that, at this precise moment, a big red flag has just gone up. I don't see it, of course; only with hindsight will the significance of this comment become clear.

"Shall we head inside, and I'll find us a little spot to have supper," he says.

"Sure," I reply, following him along a corridor and standing back as he opens his door. He pushes it open and tells me to follow him as he leads me into the room. It's dark inside, and I bash my knee against something.

"Hang on; I'll put the light on now, so you can see where you're going."

I hear him bashing and crashing as he fights along the corridor and flicks on the light switch. Light floods in, and I can see the place in all its glory. There are boxes and piles of newspapers everywhere. I mean EVERYWHERE.

"Oh, have you just moved in," I say.

"No, been here for five years," he says.

"Right. Only ...all the boxes?"

"Yes, I know - they are everywhere...come through."

I push my way through into the sitting room.

"Oh my God," I say when I get in there. The place is full of junk. I mean, it's packed with junk. I can hardly get through the door...it's completely insane. Big piles of newspapers sit around all over the floor; there are black bin bags full of cans, cartons and more newspapers. I stand and stare; I have no idea where to go, where to sit, or why on earth this is happening to me.

"Where would you like me to go?" I say.

"Do you mind if we stand?" he says. "I've got all my cartons over there. I don't want us to disrupt them, and those newspapers are from 2016, so I need to keep those."

"Why do you need to keep them?" I ask. "I mean – why do you need to keep any of this stuff?"

"Because I love it," he says. "If we could just stand here for a bit, I'll prepare the food."

He removes his jacket and takes a pile of cutlery out of his pocket.

"Cutlery is my favourite," he says, walking into the kitchen. I follow him, hoping there might be a chair in the kitchen where I can sit while he cooks, though why I don't just leave at this point is a mystery to me. How on earth can we come back from all this madness?

The kitchen is crazily packed and has about 14 times as much as the average kitchen might have in it. On the counter are eight bags of sugar, three open and five unopened. I watch as he opens the drawers, one of which is completely packed with spoons, and he carefully puts the spoons that he must have acquired from the pub into the spoon drawer. He puts the forks into the fork drawer and opens up a vegetable drawer in which the top two racks of full of newspapers, and the bottom rack is packed full of knives which tumble out when he opens the drawer. He throws the knives in, shuts them, and then turns around and jumps a little when he sees me.

"What are you doing here?" He says. "I thought you'd be relaxing in the sitting room."

"I thought I'd come and see whether you needed any help with dinner?" I say.

"You could set the table if you like," he says, moving over to the sink where he has to walk around a big bucket full of potato peelings and washes his hands. I open the drawers I've just seen him putting cutlery into and take out two forks and knives.

"What on earth are you doing?" he says.

"You asked me to lay the table…."

"Yes, but we don't use that cutlery. I like to keep that cutlery; I don't want to use it."

"Okay," I say. "Where is the cutlery that you like to use?"

"Well, if the truth be known, I don't like to use any of it. I like to keep the cutlery. I like it to be special. You can look in that carrier bag on the counter. We can use that, but please be careful with it."

I put my hand into the bag of plastic knives and forks. Again, there are loads of them. I take out two knives and two forks.

"Not those," he says. "The plain ones. Those are quite rare."

"They're plastic forks, Harry. How rare can they be?"

He glares at me before substituting the ones I chose with marginally plainer ones that he has selected.

"Can you tell me where the loo is?" I ask; I think I'll go quickly before dinner.

"Why didn't you go to the pub?" he says.

"Because I didn't need to go then."

"Would you mind walking back to the pub to the loo? There's not much room in mine."

"I'll try," I say, wander to where the bathroom appears, and open the door.

"No," shouts Harry, running after me, but it's too late. Around a hundred newspapers come tumbling out of the room.

"Oh no," he says. "Please don't touch anything. Just go to the pub if you need the loo."

That's when I think that this is nuts.

"I'm sorry about this," I say. "But I think I should get back and not stay for supper. But it was lovely to see you again."

"Why?" he says. "What's the matter?"

"Well, there's nowhere to sit or anything because of the boxes, and I don't want to have to go to the pub."

"So you're going to storm out because I like boxes and newspapers?"

As he's talking, he's putting the plastic knives and forks back into the carrier bag, and I see him visibly relax when the plastic cutlery is put away.

"Yes, I've got a bit of a headache, and I've got work early in the morning so I might head off. Sorry. Hope that's okay."

"I'm upset," he says. "You know my mother's been ill."

"Yes, I'm sorry, but I just feel awful."

I walk to the door, passed all the enormous bags full of stuff, And the boxes piled high with assorted paraphernalia; I pull the door open and turn to kiss him on the cheek.

"Sorry to be a bore," I say, before leaving, speed-walking down the path.

MISSING TED

I get to the end of the road, out of sight of his house, and sigh with relief before calling an Uber. Luckily it comes in five minutes, and I collapse into the back and immediately call Ted. It's not something I do consciously or with a great deal of planning - I find that I've called him before I know what I'm doing...it goes straight to answerphone, and I leave a message. "Hi...it's me. I...I don't know why I'm calling. I miss you. Been on the worst date ever. It was crazy. You would have laughed so much. Kept thinking of you and how mad you'd think it was...."

I hang up. I shouldn't have told Ted that I was going off on dates, but I kept imagining what he'd think about this date, roaring with laughter and hugging me and telling me he wanted me back and that I never needed to go on another date again. I felt tears spring to the corners of my eyes, then more again until I was sobbing like crazy.

"You OK, love?" asked the taxi driver nervously.

"Yes," I replied, blowing my nose in an unladylike fashion and doing a horrible snort.

My phone beeped. A text. I grabbed it...dying to see what

Ted had to say, but it was hoarder man. "Seems strange that you rushed off when we were getting along so well. So, I have a few boxes in my house. Since when was that a crime? No wonder you're single. If you apologise, I'd be happy to meet you again."

In the morning, there was a reply from Ted. "That was a bit heartless. Glad you're going on all these dates. It must be wonderful for you. Ted."

I've blown it. I've lost him forever.

SEVENTH DATE: OLLYVER,

*T*oday I'm going on a date with a guy called Ollyver. Perfectly nice name, but he spells it with two 'l's and a 'y'. Who in their right mind would distort the spelling of a perfectly respectable name like Oliver?

To make it worse, in the email that Charlie and Juan gave me, he is making quite a big deal about the fact that he wants me to spell it properly. This has got my hackles up. Surely this guy will not be another addition to the parade of ridiculousness that has passed for my experiences as an Internet dater so far.

So, I am - approaching today's date with a big dollop of scepticism.

But then, I am shocked when I spot him standing at the corner of the street, looking out and smiling when he sees me. Perhaps Ollyver, with the oddly spelt name, won't be quite such a moron after all? After all, it wasn't he who chose the spelling of the name, was it? Perhaps he has peculiar parents. We've all got those.

"I'm Mary," I say as I get close to him.

"Yes, I know," he says with a smile. "I'm Ollyver."

He's carrying a sort of doctor's bag, which gives me a small scare. Not someone else who's seen me naked? But then I realise it's more of a large document case.

"Well, it's very nice to meet you," I say, and he smiles a warm and friendly smile.

"There is quite a nice little delicatessen on the corner here which has lovely food and great coffee if you fancy it?" he says. "Then we could go for a drink later if you want. But I can't be late back because of my pets."

"Right, okay, well, the delicatessen sounds good."

I'm torn between thinking it's weird for him to announce that he has to rush back for his pets and thinking that it's quite cool that he is looking after them properly. But then I have another thought - what if the 'I have to get back for my pets' line is something he uses when he ends up on a date with someone he doesn't like?

We walk to the delicatessen, and it's lovely, as he said it would be. There are sparkly white fairy lights all around the wooden room, but with loads of lovely white ornaments on shelves, making it look clean and modern while quite funky and original. "I like this," I say.

I should say that one of the nice things about doing this Internet dating has been not only meeting a pile of new men but also going to lots of places that I would never have gone to before. This delicatessen is only a couple of miles from my home, but I've never been here. I suppose going out and meeting new people forces you to go to new places, which isn't bad.

We order their 'special cream tea', which involves not just delicious scones, homemade jam and clotted cream but a range of sandwiches and homemade cakes. It all sounds completely lovely.

While waiting for our tea to arrive, I chat with Ollyver about my day job. I've got a summary of it off pat now, having regaled the story of my life to so many would-be suitors over the past few days.

Ollyver explains that he works in a factory and is hoping to cut down his hours because he doesn't like the impact of his long hours on his pets. Once again, I feel torn between thinking this is quite odd and thinking it is quite nice to love your dog.

Our food comes on those cake stands that sit one on top of the other, with sandwiches on the bottom, a mixture of really delicious-looking cakes on the next and scones on the top with pots of jam and clotted cream.

"Enjoy," says the lady who delivers them. She has flour on her apron and looks like she has come straight from the kitchen, where she's been baking all afternoon. This is a lovely, homely place with an artistic, contemporary feel. I've slightly fallen in love with it more than with Ollyver. He is very nice, but we don't have much in common, and not being a pet owner myself, I don't think I can chat as much as he wants to about the trials and tribulations of looking after animals.

I take a big bite out of one of the sandwiches and notice that Ollyver is tearing bits of his sandwich off, so he has a pile of little bits on his plate.

Then he takes some of the small morsels and drops some into his bag.

Oh no. Red flags are everywhere; my nutter alert is flashing on full alert. Why's he doing this? What is going on? He is taking the cucumber out of the sandwiches and dropping it into his bag.

He mainly pulls out the middle of the sandwiches and drops them into his bag. He looks up and sees me staring at him.

"Everything okay?" he asks.

"Yes," I reply.

The background music in the restaurant stops for a moment before the next track comes on, and I can hear some funny noises. Then the music starts, and they disappear beneath the sound of Rod Stewart.

We carry on eating in silence, and he drops bits of food into his bag until I can sit in silence no more.

"If you don't mind me asking, why are you putting bits of the food into your bag? If you want to take the food home, we could get someone to wrap it up for you. Sorry, it's not my business; it just seems odd."

"Nothing for you to worry about," he says, looking straight at me while pulling the lettuce out of a prawn and salad sandwich and dropping it into his bag. It's as if he thinks that by keeping eye contact, I won't be able to see what's going on.

"You're doing it again," I say. "Is everything OK?"

"Of course," he replies.

Then he sighs unnecessarily loudly and lifts his bag onto the table. He opens it, and inside there are about four guinea pigs, nibbling away on the food he's provided and squeaking with appreciation.

A look of surprise must cross my face because he suddenly sounds all aggressive.

"I told you about the pets," he says. "I said I couldn't stay out long because of them."

Yes, but I thought you meant you had a dog at home. I didn't realise they were on the date with us."

"Oh no," he says. "Oh no, look what you've made them do now."

He lifts the bag as urine trickles through it onto the table and into the little pots of jam and cream before us.

"It's not my fault," I say.

"You frightened them," he counters.

"No, that's not fair," I say. "They were bound to do that. Did it not occur to you that they would do that?"

Ollyver lifts the guinea pigs out of the bag one by one (it turns out there are five) and puts them on the table. "I'm going to clean this bag out; please look after them," he says, disappearing into the men's loos.

Bloody hell.

I glance up, and everyone in the cafe is staring at me; I glance down, and the guinea pigs leave droppings across the table, nibbling at sandwiches and causing mayhem with the cream. I have no idea what to do. One starts to climb onto the cake stand, and another has climbed off the table onto one of the shelves next to us, on which there are various expensive-looking ornaments. Before I can bring down the squeaking, little furry thing, it knocks over a candle and runs to the far side. As I stand up to pick him up and bring him back onto the table, another has joined him and has nestled himself on top of a rather expensive-looking Victorian-style dish. I look back and see the two on the table still nibbling away at the sandwiches on the bottom layer of the stand.

Two?

There were five. Where the hell is the other one? I bring down the two guinea pigs from the shelf before they cause serious damage and look around for the other one. He's nowhere to be seen. There are now four guinea pigs when there should be five. They're all squeaking and squawking while a small crowd has gathered.

"I'm sorry, Madam, you can't have pets in the restaurant," says the lovely, floury owner.

"I'm sorry, they're not mine, and I seem to have lost one. Can anyone see him anywhere?"

Everyone in the restaurant is now nervously looking

around their table legs for a stray pet. But the animal can't be seen anywhere.

"I can see him," says a young boy in a red sweatshirt. "There, look…" He points at my handbag. My lovely, designer handbag. The only nice handbag I own. There's a fury head sticking up - all whiskers and tiny little chirping sounds. I put him back onto the table and zip up my handbag, thanking the boy for his help; then, I stand up and pace around the table, marshalling the animals to ensure they don't leave it.

I feel like a farmer trying to control his sheep, except farmers don't have angry diners staring at them and angry restaurant owners glaring at them while they work.

Ollyver finally returns, and a feeling of relief washes through me. Now he can take responsibility for them.

"All clean," he says, taking a handful of fresh straw from a side pocket and sprinkling it into the bag. He lifts the guinea pigs one by one and puts them back in, zipping up the top and placing the bag on the floor.

"Where were we?" he says, reaching out for a scone. The table looks like a war zone. The urine that went into the jam meant the jam is running out of its pot and all over the table. The cream has guinea pig droppings, the tablecloth is wet with urine and creamy paw prints, and guinea pig hair is everywhere. Some of the sandwiches have been nibbled at by his rodents.

"I'm full, actually," I say, standing up. I hand him £20 for my share of the food and head towards the door.

"Oh, fine," he shouts after me. "Leave if you want to…All the more for Andy, Pandy, Mandy, Sandy, Candy and me."

I glance apologetically at the owner and rush through the door. Joy of greatest joys, there's a bus just coming around the corner which goes vaguely near my house, so I jump onto it and settle into my seat, pulling out my phone to call Charlie. But when I put my hand in, the bag is wet, and the guinea pig has left me a little present in the form of two droppings on my makeup bag.

How many dates are there left to go? There can't be too many more, can there?

EIGHTH DATE: RICHARD

"*T*his one could be barefoot," says Juan with a gentle nudge.

"Oh God, why might he be barefoot?" I ask.

"Because of his occupation… He might be, that's all."

"What is his occupation? You're allowed to tell me that aren't you? Is he some Buddhist leader? Or yoga teacher or something?"

"No, actually, he is a poet. "

"Oh… That sounds interesting. A poet? I like the sound of that. I wonder whether he'll write a poem about me?"

"He might do. Though I've tried to google his poems, I can't find anything on the Internet about him. "

"So, he's not a poet, then? "

"Yes, he is; he runs poetry slams, where people go and recite their poetry, at pubs all around the place, mainly in East London… You know, Shoreditch and places like that… Hoxton… All the trendy places."

"Oh, right. Where am I meeting him?"

"You're meeting him in Richmond Park, at a little cafe

that he says inspired his greatest poem. Do you want me to come and hover in the background?"

"No - honestly, no need at all. I need to work out what on earth to wear to Richmond Park with a poet. "

"Wear whatever you want, angel; you're not trying to impress him; you're going to meet him and see whether the two of you get on. Just wear that dress that you wore when you went out with the nutty bloke with the dead wife."

"Oh, you've changed your tune. What happened to 'you have to dress up, or he won't dress up' which will mean he'll arrive with his balls hanging out."

"I've changed my mind on that now. I realise there are many fools out there, and whether you wear leggings or smart trousers won't change that. The cream dress looks lovely, though."

"Yes, I love that dress, but it hasn't brought me the greatest success. "

"Well, maybe, my dear, this will be your day."

So, I jump on the R68 bus and google "poetry slams" while the bus winds its way through Twickenham and into Richmond. Juan has given me a picture of Richard, the poet, and he looks very normal – like a bank clerk or something – I expected him to look more like Jesus, with flowing hair and an amazing beard, and maybe robes and open-toed sandals or something. Smelling of patchouli oil and wearing a look of quiet contemplation at all times.

The guy in the photo looks like the sort of guy who would deal with your gas bills or check how far overdrawn you've gone.

I arrive at the Isabella Cafe a couple of minutes early and see a man sitting on his own. He doesn't look a great deal like the guy in my picture, nor does he look like my fantasy of what a poet should look like, but he is the only guy sitting on his own, so I wander up to him.

"Hi, I'm Mary. Are you Richard?" I say. He jumps and looks at me, all alarmed.

"Yes, what do you want?" he says. The man looks terrified.

"We are supposed to be meeting for a date?"

"Are we?"

"Well, if you're Richard, and you're waiting to see someone called Mary, then – yes – we are supposed to be on a date."

"Jolly good," he says. "I'll go and get us some tea, shall I?"

"That would be lovely," I say, as he walks off towards the counter. He arrives a few minutes later with a large glass pot full of leaves, petals, and two teacups.

"This is Rose tea," he says.

It doesn't look very nice. I mean, the leaves and petals in the teapot look nice, but the colour of the water is just like urine. It doesn't look as if it will taste very nice, and I fancy a nice cup of proper tea.

"All the leaves in the tea are from flowers in the park," he says.

"Oh, that's lovely." I did like the sound of that. I'll give it a go and see what it tastes like.

"So, I hear you're a poet?" I say.

"Yes. I've always been a poet. Would you like to hear some?"

"Oh, I'd love to," I say, thinking what fun this will be.

"I'm a performance poet," he says, jumping to his feet and coughing loudly. He then proceeds to recite a poem that makes no sense at all but seems to involve him waving his arms around and whooshing like the wind before stomping and howling and shouting and then screaming and falling to the ground, shouting: 'Do not bury me. Do not bury me, good lord. Do not bury me.' The whole café has gone quiet. I look around and see that everyone is staring. The waitress has come over to check he is alright. Richard stays in his position on the floor, lying still, murmuring.

"I'm absolutely fine," he says. "The poem demands that I finish with a murmur."

"Oh," says the waitress. "Well, as long as you're alright and don't need an ambulance or anything."

"I'm fine," he says, getting to his feet.

"She ruined that a little bit, didn't she?" he says. "I didn't get to do the full murmur. Shall I do it again?"

"No," I say quickly. "The whole thing was lovely; I got to see it all, don't worry."

"Well, if you're sure," he says. And he sits down opposite me and pours us both a cup of rather nasty weak-looking tea.

"I could show you some more poems," he says. "Perhaps it would be better if you read them instead of me performing them."

"Yes, I think that would be much better," I say.

He brings out a binder full of laminated copies of his poems and asks me to read and critique them. I'm not convinced I'm going to like any of them.

"I've only ever asked one date to read my poetry," he says, as I scan through the rather miserable poems about death and the end of the world. "She said she didn't like them, so I sent her a picture of me cutting myself with blood everywhere titled, 'I bleed for you.'"

"Oh," I say. "Well, I think these poems are wonderful. All of them. You're very talented."

I haven't read them; I'm just scanning the self-indulgent dirges and pretending to think they're good to avoid any 'cutting'.

"Which is your favourite?" he asks, adding: "I'm so glad you love them."

"It's hard to say: they are all my favourites."

"But if you had to pick one."

"Oh, then the first one," I say, returning to it. 'The missions of death.'

"Ah, good choice," he says. "Shall we go for a walk through the gardens?"

"Sure," I say. Remarkably I seem to have got away with that.

The two of us head off into the gardens, and, to be fair to him, we have a nice time. It's such a beautiful park, full of bushes blooming with lipstick pink and cherry red flowers, a small brook and gorgeous wildflowers. He shows me his favourite trees and the plants he loves to come and look at every day when he's writing. He buys me ice cream, and we walk some more.

Then he tells me that the roses talk to him and the birds send him hateful messages...oh well, you can't have everything!

NINTH DATE: SAM

his whole week has been exhausting – I mean, it's just left me feeling so drained and tired I can hardly think straight. I never want to tell any strange men about my relationship history or what I'm looking for in a partner ever again.

I've now just got one more date to get through then – if Juan is right – I will either have met the man of my dreams, or I'll be very sure of what I do and don't want out of a man. I think he might be right because I've clearly established what I don't want from a man. I don't want to go on play-dates with five-year-olds; I don't want people obsessed with their dead wives, keep piles of papers in their flats or run away when they see me. Yes, a man who doesn't do that would be ideal. Oh, and a man who hasn't had his gloved hand inside me. That can't be too much to ask, surely?

Maybe today's date will provide a man who becomes my life partner. Hmmm! Well, it's worth trying anyway. The guy I am meeting is called Sam; he describes himself as "big and cuddly" and wants to meet a woman like him. I think that description fits me like a glove, so hopefully, we'll get on. We are meeting at a bar in the middle of Kingston, which I'm not keen on, but we're going to the cinema afterwards, so it makes perfect sense.

I push my way into the Kings Tonne pub and through the crowds of young people (by "young", I mean "underage"). When I get to the bar, I see a gorgeous big man with a lovely, wide smiling face looking at me.

"Wow! You must be Mary," he says. And I feel a rush of attraction for the first time in this internet dating experience. Many of the guys I've met have been nice, but I haven't fancied any of them. This guy, though - he's nice. He reminds me a little bit of Ted, but I try to push that to the back of my mind. He's got a lovely open face and big shiny eyes and looks genuinely thrilled to see me.

"And you must be Sam," I say, smiling back at him as he grabs me in a big bear hug.

"What can I get you to drink then, gorgeous?" he says, and I feel like all these ridiculous dates I've had have been worth it – here is a genuinely lovely guy. He picks up our drinks and heads over to the table on the far side.

"After you," he says, as we head over to a table that he has reserved by throwing his jacket and jumper across them. We sit down with our drinks. "Sorry to make you lead the way, but I wanted to sneakily look at you as you walked. I didn't expect you to be so gorgeous," he says. "I love the way you are dressed."

He looks me up and down as he talks, and I blush under his intense gaze.

"You look lovely, too," I say, slightly embarrassed now.

He is still appraising me as his eyes alight on my shoes. I've got cream open-toe sandals on, not very high – just kitten heels, but he likes them a lot.

"You have such beautiful feet. I love your shoes," he says.

"Thank you." I'm not sure what else to say.

"And that colour on your toenails," he adds. Then he looks at my face and can see that I'm feeling quite awkward.

"Sorry," he says. "You look great. But I've already said that haven't I? I'll stop saying it now."

We finish our drinks while chatting about what's happening in the news, friends we have, and places we both know. We do that thing of talking about places we know and trying to work out whether we've both been there at the same time. Then we decide to have another drink even though it's almost time for the cinema. "We'll have to drink this one fast," he says, standing up and heading for the bar.

"I'll get these," I say.

"No, you won't. You stay there. I'll be back in a minute."

He heads to the bar while I sit there and watch him, smiling at how nice he is. I'm dying to tell Juan and Dave how complimentary he's being. The two of them have said a few times that they think men would get on much better with women if they just gave them compliments every so often.

"Here we go," he says, putting my drink on the table. He has enormous, hairy hands and is quite tanned. He looks almost Mediterranean with his glossy black hair but says he was born in Manchester, and his parents moved down south when he was young.

"Why don't you swing round and face me," he says, pulling my chair around, so I'm facing him next to me rather the table in front. I'm very impressed that he can swing me around like that. I notice his eyes have moved down my legs, and he's staring at my feet again. He loves my shoes; it's bizarre.

"I'll try and get some in your size if you want," I say, and he bursts out laughing.

"I don't think the shoes would look half as nice with my

big hairy ugly feet. I like your feet...they are all soft and fleshy and lovely."

Fleshy? Really? Is that a good word? It seems like the most bizarre word to use.

"Okay, come on then, we have to neck these," he says. "The film starts in 10 minutes, and we are five minutes from the cinema. Are you ready?"

"I'm ready," I say, and we both down our drinks straight away. I've only got a small glass of wine, but he's got a pint of beer, so he has the biggest struggle, but he seems to do it OK... knocking the drink back and standing up with an appreciative grunt. "Come on then, let's go."

At the cinema, I step in front of him and head to the counter.

"I'm buying the tickets," I say. "You bought all the drinks."

"Too late," he declares. "I bought them this morning. Here you go...."

He holds out tickets, not just for the normal cinema seats, but for the posh seats in the row with the lovely velvety backs that cost extra.

"Oh, you're spoiling me," I say, and he gives me a gentle squeeze as we walk towards screen two.

The auditorium's quite busy, but as usual, no people are sitting in the posh seats, so we walk up to them and take our places, sitting in splendid isolation on our velvet thrones.

"This is nice," he says."We've got the row to ourselves. I hope I can trust you to keep your hands off me."

"Ha ha ha," I say, tucking my handbag under my seat and stretching my legs out in front. "It's lovely. Having all this room is great," I say.

"Yes, I love it when you stretch your legs like that."

"You're not going to stop going on about my shoes again, are you?"

"It's not your shoes that entice me; your feet. I love women's feet, and yours are amazing."

"Oh, right," I say. What else can you say? What on earth do you say to a man who says that?

"Would you mind if I removed your shoes?" he whispers as the lights go down and the screen flickers to life, asking people to turn off their mobile phones.

"I think I'll just leave them on," I say.

"Please," he says. "I did buy all the drinks, and the cinema ticket, the least you could do is let me touch your feet. "

"You're making me feel awkward," I say. "Can we watch the film and stop talking about my feet."

"But they're so beautiful. I just love larger ladies with painted toenails. It drives me wild."

While the adverts dance across the screen, telling us of films are coming soon, I sit there, nervously, with my feet tucked under, while Sam sits there peering down at the bits of my feet he can see.

"It should be against the law to hide feet as gorgeous as that," he says. "Beautiful, sexy feet should be seen, not tucked away."

I decide to ignore him and concentrate on the film, but I have to tell you that it's very hard to ignore a man who insists on going on and on and on about your feet.

The film starts, and we fall into a companionable silence. Thank God. He's stopped the fat lady foot fetish for a moment.

But...not for long. Just as I've forgotten about his madness and am starting to enjoy the film, he starts shuffling about and drops his keys on the floor.

"Excuse me," he says, clambering down and fishing around for them. "They're here somewhere."

Then I feel my toes getting wet. What's happening? I look down, and he's sucking my toes through my shoes. Sucking my toes! Have you ever had that happen to you while you're in the cinema? No, you haven't. And you know why - because you haven't been internet dating with a mad chubby chaser. And neither will I. EVER AGAIN. I kick out to push him off and end up booting him rather sharply in the face.

"Ahhh…" he cries, standing up. "What is wrong with you?"

"What is wrong with me?" I ask. "The question is - what is wrong with you? What nutter starts sucking a woman's toes through her shoes in the cinema?"

"It's what I like doing," he says, sounding pitiful now. We're standing there in the lobby; blood is running down his face.

"You should go to the hospital," I say. "I'm going home."

And I turn and walk out of the door.

NINE DATES IN TWO WEEKS, BUT WHAT HAVE WE LEARNED?

I am sitting, a glass of wine in hand, back in my flat, tucked up in the armchair while Dave, Juan and Charlie sit opposite on the sofa, open-mouthed as I recall the events of the evening.

Dave looks at Juan, then at Charlie: "What sort of characteristics were you looking for when you set up these dates?" he asks. "I mean – every one of them has been operating at a whole new level of bonkers."

"Yeah," says Juan, scratching his head. "They all seemed like nice guys on paper."

"The police should sign you up when they are looking for people who have committed particularly insane crimes – you'd find them in a heartbeat. You have a madman detector of some sort."

"Yeah," he says again. "I don't know what to say. I feel awful."

"Hey, don't worry – it was fine," I say. "It was a huge learning experience."

"Yep – you learned never to let Juan pick out dates for you again."

"No – come on – it's not Juan's fault. There are a lot of nutters out there."

"Yes, but – honestly – to get that many lunatics – one after the other…date after date. That's odd."

"It's unfair to say they were all lunatics. The first guy was completely nice; he just hadn't gotten over his wife."

"I'm sure there are a lot of guys out there who lose their wives and struggle to get over it – but they don't take future dates on a pilgrimage to see where she died."

"But I don't think he meant it like that: he didn't mean it in a threatening or angry way; we'd just been talking about it, and we happened to be passing it, so he pointed it out."

"No, Mary, that's not true…he turned completely the wrong way at the roundabout to take you there, and you had to ask him to take you home. Dead Wife Darren is a nutter – plain and simple. Don't you agree, Juan?"

"It's very hard to disagree when you put it like that," he says sheepishly.

"Which guy came next?" asks Dave.

"The guy who ran away," I say.

"Well – he was just rude," says Juan. "A horrible, rude man."

"Yes – he was rude rather than mad," says Dave. "But I did enjoy the descriptions of him legging it like Usain Bolt while Juan screamed obscenities after him. Well done, Juan. I wish I'd been there to support you."

The two men high-five one another and ask me which date came after that.

"Oh – that was Martin who took me on a playdate. Remember him?"

"I remember all the little boys crying when you left because they enjoyed playing Action Man games with you. And – yes, he was mad, but it was Harry the hoarder after that – and he was all your doing," Juan says to me. "That one was nothing to do with me."

"I accept full responsibility for that particular nutter," I say. "I still can't get over what his flat was like – there must have been about 30 piles of newspapers, some of the ones in the corridor went up to the ceiling. And the cutlery...I've never known anyone get so excited about cutlery. It was weird on a whole new scale. But he'd seemed so nice and normal until we returned to his place. That was very odd and very disappointing."

I get up and top everyone's glasses up while Charlie tries to work out who was next. "Oh, it was Ollyver with his guinea pigs," she says, looking up from the printouts in front of her. "There was no sign of him being a nutter on his profile. It mentions pets in the 'things I like section', but it doesn't say that he'll be taking his guinea pigs with him or anything...he doesn't even mention his pets in the main piece he's written about himself; it just appears at the end. It's bizarre.

"That was the only date I felt uncomfortable," I say. "On most of them, I got out of there quickly before it became a mad disaster, but when those guinea pigs were all over the table, and he went to the loo to wash his bag out, I swear to God, I don't think I've ever felt so much pressure in my life before – they were running everywhere, causing chaos. And he just wanted to carry on afterwards like nothing had happened, even though guinea pig droppings were all over the bloody food."

"Richard, the poet, was after that, then the mad chubby chaser."

"Richard was fine," I say. "He just loved to perform poetry. I didn't fancy him at all, and he didn't fancy me, but when we went for a walk, it was nice because he knew all the names of the trees and flowers and had lots of stories about historical encounters in the park. I enjoyed that date once he'd stopped going on about his poems."

"And the madman at the end?"

"Yep, tonight was odd. I kicked him hard, you know. I didn't mean to, but he took me by such surprise I lashed out. I wouldn't be surprised if I broke his nose."

"Serves him right," says Dave. "Bloody idiot."

Charlie and Juan have been quiet during this conversation, except to defend themselves occasionally.

"It was all fun, though. Thank you for trying. Here's to great friends who try to help you meet someone…."

I raise my glass, and Dave raises his, adding: "Even if the men they fix you up with are stark, staring mad." Then Juan and Charlie glance at one another and tentatively raise their glasses.

"I think I may have cocked up a bit," says Juan, lowering his head.

"No, don't be silly, I'm fine," I say. "It was good fun; we're only joking."

"No, not about the dates per se," he says. "I mean about something else that I have planned."

There's a sort of silence because if he's not embarrassed about the dates, but he is embarrassed about something else he's planned, then this something else must be quite special.

"What have you done?" I say, looking at both of them.

"Well, we've kind of organised something for Saturday night."

"What have you organised for Saturday night?"

"A party."

"Oh, that's nice."

"Yes," says Charlie. "Only I now think it's maybe not very

nice. It may be the most stupid idea ever. We thought of having a little get-together because of Juan leaving and everything, but then we got a bit carried away…."

"What have you done?" I ask.

"Well, we've invited everyone you dated to it."

"You what?"

"Sorry. We didn't think they'd all be as mad as they have been. We've sent them all invitations to a party at Charlie's house on Saturday."

Dave looks like he'll explode with surprise and sheer incomprehension; Charlie looks sheepish, and Juan looks around the room, refusing to meet anyone's eye.

A party at which all the nutters that I have dated over the past week will be altogether…hoarder, sprinter, toe sucker and poet. And will there be guinea pigs and a 5-year-old child there?

Bloody hell, this is insane.

"There's something else we need to tell you," says Charlie.

"What?"

"Ted is seeing someone."

"Ted? What, my Ted?"

"Yes, I'm sorry, angel. I bumped into Veronica, who said she saw him with Michella from Fat Club in the pub near him. I don't know whether it's serious, but I thought I should tell you."

Charlie keeps talking, but I don't hear anything else. I feel like I've been shot. It's like I'm falling through the gaps in the universe. My head is spinning, and I can't get enough air into my lungs. Has someone turned off the oxygen?

Suddenly the party feels neither here nor there. I don't care whether there's a party or not. I couldn't give a flying fuck whether those losers are congregating or not. I just want Ted.

"But I love him," I say, standing up and heading to my bedroom before the tears come. "I love him as I've never loved anyone before."

THE PARTY TO END ALL PARTIES

*I*t's a difficult couple of days after hearing about Ted. I feel like I'm existing in a different reality from everyone else… I'm operating on the torn edges of life…all meandering and vague. I awake in the early hours of the morning and am desperate to sleep in the afternoons: it's as if I've just been on a long-distance flight. I don't know what to do with myself; my mind whirrs so much that it hurts, and images of Ted and the great times we've had together flash aggressively into my mind suddenly and without warning. I find myself relying on the kindness of Juan and Charlie during these difficult early days, as they spend hours talking to me and making sure I'm able to function while my heart has been torn to shreds.

I tell them to go ahead with the party because I can't face telling them to cancel it. It feels easier to go ahead with everything and somehow cope with it than to make a drama about stopping it.

So, the day arrives, and I am determined to put my

broken heart to one side and try to enjoy myself: this is Juan's going away party, and there's every chance that none of the daters will turn up. It could be just a few of us drinking wine and celebrating our friendship.

If they do turn up, it will be the most ridiculous party ever to be thrown. Honestly, I think people will be talking about this party in 10 years and declaring it to be the most absurd ever staged. How can it possibly work out well if they come? I mean, on what level is this a good idea? I don't want to meet anyone of these men ever in my life again, and they will all be there tonight.

I also don't want my friends to bear witness to the wild collection of grossly inappropriate men that I have been dating for the past few weeks. What would have been a cringe-worthy personal embarrassment is now to be turned into a huge spectacle for everyone to witness.

I think Juan is still amazed that I allowed the party to take place. Bizarrely, if it hadn't been for discovering that Ted was dating Michela, I probably wouldn't have. But that news wounded me so badly and destabilised me to such an extent that I feel nothing can hurt me now.

"Are you OK?" Juan asks me for the 1000th time, and I tell him I'm fine.

"Oh, you are such a gorgeous woman. I knew you'd respond to this properly."

"I'm not sure I'm responding 'properly'," I say. "I still think it will be a ridiculous party."

"It depends on what you mean by "ridiculous party," I think the ridiculous parties are the best parties."

"Well, this one should be a belter then," I say.

At 7 pm, we head to Charlie's place – we are all glammed up and ready to party. Juan is in a sparkly striped suit that is extremely tight. He looks magnificent, of course, even if his hair is all standing on end, making him look as if he's been lifted out of a well by his ankles.

"You need more lipstick," he says. "I'm going to be your beauty consultant for the evening."

I notice that Juan is wearing makeup himself. He is wearing eyeliner which he insists on calling "guyliner", and definitely has foundation on, even though he denies it. He produces a gorgeous cherry red lipstick that Charlie handed him and proceeds to apply it. I'm sure I look like a bloody clown, but there's too much else to worry about with the prospect of the attendees at the party tonight, so I just let him put it on me.

Charlie looks gorgeous, I mean – really lovely. She's wearing a cream sheath dress with bare legs that look tanned and glossy. They look so long and elegant with her high, gold, strappy sandals. They're so high that if I wore them for more than five minutes, I'd be flat on my face, but I'm confident that Charlie will be striding around the party looking like a supermodel.

I'm already starting to regret offering to take her on my free trip to Saint Lucia. I can't imagine how gorgeous she will look in a bikini and how correspondingly awful I will look.

"You look like Marilyn Monroe with that lipstick on," said Charlie; I smile at her and don't offer the retort that Marilyn Monroe has been dead for about 50 years. Instead, I smile and thank her, and we walk sheepishly out of the flat.

"Gosh, you must be nervous about this," said Charlie. "You've normally given me a real ear bashing for telling me you look like a dead actress."

"I did think it," I admit. "But decided, for the first time in my life, to keep my thoughts to myself. I guess I am getting a bit nervous. I might have to pull a Usain Bolt and run out of there when people start coming.

"IT'S VERY nice of you to host this," I say to Charlie, and she drapes her arm over my shoulder as we walk down the path to her flat.

"You're very welcome."

"Do you think any of the mad daters will turn up?"

"I think some will," she replies.

"What about Usain Bolt?"

"Who?"

"You know, the guy who ran away at the speed of light as soon as he saw me."

"Oh blimey, Usain. Yes. I don't know. I wouldn't have thought so after the abuse we gave him."

"You know this is the most ridiculous idea ever, don't you?"

"Yes," says Charlie. "When we thought of it, we imagined you going on lots of light, friendly dates and not being sure who you liked best, so we thought that if we invited them all to a party, you'd be able to decide. We never once imagined that there would be so many nutters."

"Oh well - the party comes from a good place, from Juan's warped and ridiculous mind and Charlie's kind heart. So, I will go with it. Maybe we could have a sign, and if I'm talking to someone driving me nuts, I could signal to you somehow?"

"Good plan," said Dave, appearing at my side. "Maybe just bash your hands on your head and squeal or something?"

"I think it might call something more subtle than that. Maybe I'll wiggle my ear lobe. Let's do that."

"Okay, that's a good plan."

There is a loud banging on the door just as I'm about to go into detail about the ear-wiggling thing. My heart beats a little faster, and I push past Charlie into the kitchen and pour myself the largest glass of wine imaginable.

"Don't worry, it's only Dave," shouts Juan. "You can put the cyanide down."

It's a bizarre thing, but part of me is embracing the madness of all this as a huge distraction from the pain of Ted having found someone new. I felt strangled by the knowledge that he has a girlfriend a couple of days ago, but the riotous ludicrousness of this party is filling my mind and stopping the darker thoughts from entering it. I'm grateful that it's going on, even though I'm dreading seeing these bizarre men again.

The first date to arrive at the party is Martin. Dave looks at me quizzically, and I mouth: "play date". He puts his thumbs up in recognition that he now realises that this guy took me on a date to a toddler's cafe party and left me playing games with the children while he chatted to the mums until Charlie and Juan turned up to rescue me.

"Lovely to see you again," he says, kissing me gently on either cheek and shaking hands with the others when I introduce them.

"I remember you from the cafe," he says to Juan. "Why did you have to leave so suddenly, Mary?"

"Well, it was a bit odd," I say. "You know – going for a playdate with children when we were supposed to be on a date."

"Yes, but I had a son. I said in my profile that I had a son. He's part of the package. I didn't want to leave him at home. Sorry – but I thought it would work as a simple, relaxed first date."

"Yes, but – it was hard for us to talk properly."

"I know. I suppose I thought those serious face-to-face dinners when you first know someone can be so intense. We might have fun if we bonded over Lego or something. I thought that if we got on in a relaxed environment like that, we could go out more formally later. But you just rushed off."

"Yes, because it all seemed so odd."

"I'm sorry you found it odd. It's completely my fault; I misjudged everything. Still, it's lovely to be invited to meet with you again."

"Yes, you too," I say.

Well, maybe that one wasn't a nutter after all.

As I'm standing there, enjoying this man's company in a way that I never expected to, it dawns on me that I don't know whether he knows that I went on lots of internet dates, and they have all been invited tonight.

"Do excuse me," I say, introducing him to Dave and asking Dave whether he would get him a drink.

I walk over to Juan and take him aside. "Do these men know that there will be lots of men at this party that I have dated?" I say.

"Of course not," replies Juan. "Why would I tell them that?"

"Because when they find out, they might be cross?"

"Well, tough, they haven't been exactly the most glorious with men. This party is for you, not them."

As Juan and I talk, I see Ollyver arrive. He has a bag with him, which immediately makes me panic. The last thing we need here are guinea pigs running all over the flat. Behind him comes Harry, the guy who had seemed so lovely when I met him in the bar and then great over lunch, but then thoroughly weird in his flat – with his piles of newspapers, boxes and boxes of rubbish, and general weirdness about cutlery. He comes in and stands with his hands on his hips, surveying the scene. Then he sees me and walks over.

"Thanks for inviting me," he says. "I was very surprised to be invited to a party. I thought I might have blown it with the text I sent."

"Of course not; we can be friends," I say. But inside, I'm thinking 'blew it with the text? Mate, you blew it well before the text."

I introduce him to Juan, and the two men shake hands before he wanders into the kitchen to get a drink. Juan turns to me.

"He seems nice," he says." Which one was he? Why didn't you like him?"

He is the one I met in the pub, remember, the one who is a hoarder."

"Oh yes, I remember now," says Juan. "It's a shame – nice guy. Good firm handshake. He's quite strong."

"Yes, from lifting all those damn newspapers."

I walk into the kitchen to get a refill and stumble across the oddest of scenes.

Martin holds Ollyver's guinea pig while Ollyver fills up Harry's glass. Of course, it's only a matter of time until one of them says, "so, how do you know Mary?" And the whole thing will implode, and they will realise what this party is all about. I look over at Dave and give him a warm smile; I think I might need him to get me safely out of here if things kick off.

Next into the fray is Dead Wife Darren, arriving just before Rupert, my gynaecologist. Now it's getting weird. If anyone asks him how he knows me, I'm unsure whether he'll say, "I'm her gynaecologist," or "I met her on a blind date." Either is ridiculous, but I think the former is more ridiculous, so I hope he says we went on a date.

I look over at Charlie and realise she's talking to someone I vaguely know. It's one of the date men, but I can't figure out which one it is, especially since he has bandages across his face. It looks like he's been in a nasty accident.

"Well, this is very nice. Thank you very much for inviting me," says Rupert, forcing me to spin around. I smile at him, and we exchange kisses on the cheek. "I thought I'd never see you again," he says.

"Well, not until my next smear test, eh?"

"It's unlikely to be me that does it," he says. "You know, you really shouldn't worry quite so much about my occupation. I'm a nice guy. We seem to get on well. I didn't quite understand why you ran away."

"You didn't understand?"

"Well, I did; I didn't think there was any need for it. We could've had another drink and carried on chatting."

"I just felt so embarrassed," I said. It was at that point that I remembered who it was that Charlie was talking to. The chubby chaser. The rather rampant and unashamedly foot-obsessed lunatic, and now I remembered why he was all bandaged up. I kicked him in the face. Goodness, I forgot all about that.

I look over at him and Charlie and see him looking down at her lovely feet, all on show in her gold open-toe sandals. Oh, God. Charlie is very slender, so it wouldn't appeal to his chubby chasing but might appeal to him on the foot front. You can practically see all of her feet. What on earth was she thinking of?

"I'm just going to pop over and check Charlie is okay," I say to Rupert. "It's lovely to see you again."

I walk over to Charlie and Charlie, who have already worked out that they share the same name and are laughing about it while clinking glasses. "I'm glad you two have met," I say to Charlie "female".

"How is your nose, Charlie," I say to him. "I'm sorry I

accidentally kicked you in the face. It was entirely an accident."

There is a small gasp from Charlie as she realises who this is, and she disappears.

I turn back to Charlie. "Seriously, how is your face?"

"Feeling much better now, thank you very much," he says. "I'm sorry about the way I behaved. It was unforgivable. The main reason I came today was to apologise and tell you that I was completely out of order."

But, as we're talking, I notice his gaze stray to the other side of the room. I follow the direction that his eyes are moving to and see that the ladies from Fat Club have arrived. This must be an absolute paradise to our resident chubby chaser.

"They are my friends, Charlie," I say. "Just try and be normal and friendly, please."

"Of course I will," he says. "I have already explained that my behaviour before was an aberration. Totally out of character." But then he pushes past me and makes a beeline for the chubbiest ladies at the party.

I'm standing there alone when Rupert appears again. "Is it your birthday today?" he says. "Or just holding a party because it's almost your birthday,"

"Yeah, because it's almost my birthday," I say. "And because Juan is going back to Spain soon, we thought we'd get a few people together."

"Oh, I see," he says. "I assumed that Juan was your brother; is that not the case."

I look over at Juan, who weighs less than my arm and has a distinctively Mediterranean look. I'm a fat English lady with rosy cheeks and highlighted blonde hair. It's hard to imagine two people looking less similar. I've no idea how anyone on earth could think we were brother and sister.

"He's a friend I met on holiday," I say. "A lovely guy. We stayed in touch."

I start to stroke my ear, worried that Rupert will think I'm interested if I hang around him too long. He's a nice guy, but I swear I can't possibly date my gynaecologist. It's too weird. And…the undeniable truth is - I don't fancy him in the least.

My ear rubbing brings Charlie to my side, but then the two of us hear a small commotion and Dave's raised voice. "What the fuck?" he shouts before there is a scream from Veronica, one of my friends from Fat Club, and the sound of people scampering out of the kitchen.

"She's got rats," says Veronica, tossing her glossy dark hair over her shoulders and fleeing the room. "Your friend has got rats."

"I bloody haven't," says Charlie, who has never taken much to Veronica. She storms into the kitchen, and there's the sound of raised voices before Charlie pops her head back out again: "It's that mad bastard with his guinea pigs," she says. "They are running all around the kitchen.

"Oh, God."

I head into the kitchen to help Charlie and stumble upon a scene I never expected to witness. Harry the hoarder and Martin Playdate are on their hands and knees, crawling around with Ollyver, trying to catch his squeaking pets.

"There, over by you," shouts Harry. "In that corner, right next to your knee. Have you got it?"

"Yes, got it," says Martin, standing up and holding the fluffy little animal aloft like it's the World Cup.

"Ah, it's Candy," says Harry, taking her off Martin and putting her straight into his bag. "I think Candy is my favourite. She understands me in a way that the others don't. But then she's older than they are."

"Right," says Harry. "Well, I'm glad she's safely back with you then."

"How many are there?" I say, noticing that the men have got back onto their hands and knees and are still searching. "And why do you have to take them wherever you go."

"Because I don't like to leave them at home all day on their own," he replies aggressively. "Two escaped; one has just been returned to the fold, meaning one is still missing."

"Got it," says Martin. "I'm good at this, aren't I? Really good at it."

"Yes, very good," I reply. Perhaps he should put 'guinea pig catcher' on his CV?

"Oh, hello, what have we got here?" says Richard, the poet, striding in and observing the scene. "I didn't realise it was a 'bring a rat' party."

"It's not a rat," shout Ollyver and Charlie at the same time, with Charlie adding: "I don't have rats in my house, OK?"

"OK," says Richard. "OK, no rats… Good for you. I have a poem about small animals, actually. Let me recite it for you."

Now, as we know, Richard can't just recite a poem, so as soon as he says this, I know there's going to be an over-the-top performance. But I don't anticipate anything like what follows.

Richard jumps up so he is standing on top of the table under which the guinea pig hunters have been conducting their search.

"Be careful; you might fall."

"No, I won't. This table and I are friends. I regard gravity as an impertinent con trick unworthy of being taken seriously."

And, with that, he begins his dramatic tale.

"Mini monsters, scary faces, long of hair, in creepy places."

Then he pauses, jumps up, landing noisily on the table,

and shouts at the top of his voice: "OH YOU EVIL, FECK-LESS, MEANINGLESS OTHERS. ALL TO DAMNATION – CRATURES AND MOTHERS."

He's howling now, really howling, and all of the men in the party are in the kitchen, trying to work out what's happening.

Charlie and I are madly twirling our earlobes.

"Enough," shouts Dave. "We'd like you to leave now."

The men who have conducted themselves appropriately assume this instruction isn't meant for them, but it is. We're done with this. Done with online dating, done with bonkers parties. Done with it all.

LIFE WITHOUT TED

*O*nce they have gone, I flop onto Charlie's sofa and silently sit there.

"Do you think we were too hasty there," says Juan. "You know – chucking them out like that."

"No," Charlie and Dave chorus. "We had to get them out. That poet is from another planet."

"Yeah, he's OK when he's not reciting his poems," I say, offering a weak defence of him. "When we walked in Richmond Park, he was lovely, but those poems he writes…and his need to perform them…Jesus – that's hard-core."

"With hindsight, the party wasn't a great idea, was it?" says Juan.

"Even without hindsight," I say. And that's when we all start laughing.

"How are you feeling, Mary?" asks Charlie.

"I'm OK," I say. "I feel exhausted. And sad, of course. I'm sad I cocked things up so badly with Ted."

"You're assuming you cocked things up. You don't know that. Why don't you call him and see how he feels." says Charlie.

"Yes," I say, but it's breaking me in two that he might be with Michela. I don't want to call him and be brutally rejected by him.'

"We need a plan to win him back," says Charlie. "Pass me that notebook. We are making a plan right now."

WANT TO READ MORE ABOUT MARY BROWN?

The next book is called **Mary Brown in Lockdown**, and it is the story of how Mary puts together a six-week campaign to win back Ted. But then...lockdown hits, and she's stuck at home with Juan, eating cakes, talking to the pigeons & making a giant fool of herself on GMTV. Once lockdown is over, it's time to try and find Ted. Will he take her back?

ALSO BY BERNICE BLOOM

There are lots more Mary Brown books in the series.
They can all be found on Amazon.

THE ORDER OF THE MARY BROWN BOOKS:

1. WHAT'S UP, MARY BROWN?
2. THE ADVENTURES OF MARY BROWN
3. CHRISTMAS WITH MARY BROWN
4. MARY BROWN IS LEAVING TOWN
5. MARY BROWN IN LOCKDOWN
6. MYSTERIOUS INVITATION
7. A FRIEND IN NEED
8. DOG DAYS FOR MARY BROWN
9. DON'T MENTION THE HEN WEEKEND
10. THE ST LUCIA MYSTERY

THE ORDER OF THE SUNSHINE COTTAGE BOOKS:

1. RETURN TO SUNSHINE COTTAGE
2. GIRLS AT SUNSHINE COTTAGE
3. VALENTINE'S DAY AT SUNSHINE COTTAGE
4. LIFE AT SUNSHINE COTTAGE
5. CHRISTMAS AT SUNSHINE COTTAGE
6. SUMMER AT SUNSHINE COTTAGE

Printed in Great Britain
by Amazon